Sasha's
Spending Spree

PATRINA McKENNA

Publisher: Patrina McKenna

patrina.mckenna@outlook.com

ISBN-13: 978-1-8381827-6-2

DEDICATION

For my family and friends

1

PROMOTION PROSPECTS

Twenty-two-year-old Sasha sighed as she rummaged through her wardrobe. She always wore the same two outfits for work: black trousers with either a white or cream blouse. She alternated the blouses each day so that some weeks she wore the cream one three times and then the next week she only wore it twice. Sasha was sure that no one even noticed her office attire. They were all too busy. Working in a call centre was non-stop from nine to five – that's if you were lucky enough to get a job on the day shift.

Chloe popped her head around Sasha's bedroom door. 'If you want to borrow my pink jacket tomorrow, you're more than welcome. It would work well with the white blouse and black trousers.'

Before Sasha could speak, Kerstin squeezed past Chloe and stood before their friend, holding out a navy knee-length dress. 'This will be more suitable for an interview. When you get the team leader position, you'll be able to afford some new clothes.' Kerstin nudged Chloe. 'You've got some nude ankle boots Sasha could borrow, haven't you?'

Chloe smiled. 'I certainly have.'

Sasha frowned. 'I feel so bad borrowing things from you two, but at the moment, I can just about afford my share of the rent.'

Chloe hugged Sasha. 'We know. You've not been as lucky as us with finding a well-paid job so quickly after university. The call centre is just a stopgap for you. This promotion will ease the pain until you find a more suitable position. At least we've managed to all stay together by renting this apartment in London. It's such a step up from the student accommodation we shared for three years.'

Sasha lowered her eyes. It wasn't the first time she wondered if she'd done the right thing by leaving home and moving in with the girls. Her finances would have been easier if she'd returned to Durham to live with her mother until she found a better job. Still, she'd made her choice. It was critical the interview tomorrow went well.

Sasha's phone rang, and a smile lit up her face. 'Sorry, girls. I need to take this. I've been waiting for a call from Grandpa Wilf all day.'

Chloe and Kerstin exited Sasha's room and closed the door behind them. Sasha sat down on her bed and accepted the call. 'Grandpa! How are things? Are you settling in well?'

Grandpa Wilf sounded as cheery as usual, 'I'm not doing too badly. I've made some friends already. Also, do you remember that posh gent who lived in the big house at the bottom of my garden? Well, you'd never believe it; we lived over the fence from one another for over thirty years and never spoke. Now we're in the same care home in apartments next to each other.'

Sasha smiled. 'How lovely! What's his name?'

'Rupert.'

Sasha giggled. 'Like the bear?'

Grandpa Wilf chuckled. 'Well, he doesn't wear checked trousers, if that's what you mean. He's better turned out than me, though. He wore a suit to dinner last night. The last time I wore a suit was at your mother's wedding, and that one was hired from some posh fancy place. Your father insisted I wore a pink waistcoat. It clashed with my eyes. Talking of your father, have you heard from him recently?'

'No. He's not worth mentioning.'

Sasha could hear her grandfather sigh down the phone. 'That's a shame. He's missing out on seeing you blossom into a fine young woman. How's your job going in the big city?'

'It's going well, Grandpa. I'm hoping to get a promotion tomorrow.'

'Will that mean more money?'

'Yes, lots more money. When that happens, I'll buy a train ticket to visit Durham to see you. You can introduce me to Rupert.'

'That would make my day, pet.'

Sasha's heart melted every time her grandfather called her that. She missed him so much. She swallowed hard. 'Anyway, I must go now, Grandpa. I love you. Speak soon.'

*

The following morning, Sasha sat across the desk from the Call Centre Manager. Margaret was a formidable woman. 'Tell me why I should make you team leader?'

Sasha squeezed her hands together in her lap. 'I know I'm only twenty-two, and this is my first job since leaving university, but I love working here and have much to offer.'

Margaret leaned on the desk and stared into Sasha's eyes. 'You're wet behind the ears.'

Sasha held up her hand to touch an ear, and Margaret laughed. 'You don't even know the meaning of that saying. How will you lead a team of skilled call operators without experience? You university graduates think you're the bee's knees.'

Sasha's jaw dropped as a redness crept up her neck before exploding onto her face. She had to keep composed, even though she wanted to tell Margaret where to stick her job. Sasha stood up. 'Well, I'm very sorry for wasting your time. I'll get back to my desk straight away.'

Margaret shook her head. 'Sit down. There's someone I want you to meet.' Margaret made a call on her phone, 'It's OK to come up now.'

Within minutes, Margaret's office door opened to the sight of a tanned, blue-eyed young man with dark blonde hair who headed straight for Margaret before kissing her on the cheek.

Margaret smiled at Sasha. 'You didn't waste my time by applying for the team leader role. You gave me an idea. Meet my son, Lawrence. He's another university graduate who thinks he's God's gift to employers.'

Lawrence held out his hand to shake Sasha's while

flashing a cheeky grin. 'I'm very pleased to meet you. Please call me Lawrie.'

Margaret continued to divulge her thoughts to Sasha, 'The difference between you and my son is that he's just taken a gap year to travel the world, hence the tan. He's also still living with his mother, so isn't in any hurry to find a job.' Margaret slid a cutting glance at the grinning young man. 'Anyway, my son now has an unpaid work experience placement at this company. Lawrence is your new Team Leader. He will be learning on the job.'

Lawrie stopped grinning. 'Unpaid!? You didn't mention that.'

Margaret sniffed. 'You have free accommodation and a monthly allowance which will more than cover your social costs while you get to grips with being employed. A year should do it. After that, I expect you to flee the nest and stand on your own two feet.'

Sasha gulped; it was now Lawrie whose cheeks were ablaze.

Margaret waved an arm at Sasha. 'You can get back to work now. I will introduce Lawrence to the rest of the team.'

2

BAD NEWS

Chloe and Kerstin were shocked. Kerstin decided to open the bottle of champagne anyway. 'It's nepotism! It shouldn't be allowed. Family favouritism has no place in business.'

Sasha sighed as she took hold of the glass of champagne Kerstin held out for her. 'Well, I can't compete with someone working for free for the next year.'

Chloe raised her champagne glass in the air. 'We need to celebrate something.'

Sasha's phone rang. It was Grandpa Wilf. 'Did you get the promotion?'

Sasha cringed. 'Not this time, Grandpa. It will take me a little longer to save enough money for a train ticket. I'll do it, though. I promise to be up to see you before Christmas.'

It was Grandpa Wilf's turn to sigh. 'That's over six months away. I'll not be having that, pet. Just leave things with me.' Grandpa Wilf ended the call and reached for his wallet. He took out a ten-pound note and placed it in an envelope. He'd post it to Sasha in the morning. She'd be up to see him before long.

Sasha smiled. 'Let's have a toast to Grandpa Wilf. I don't know what I'd do without him.'

The girls giggled as they held their glasses in the air. 'To Grandpa Wilf!'

*

Two days later, the money from Durham arrived for Sasha. Her heart sank. She couldn't get to Durham and back for ten pounds. Chloe and Kerstin sensed Sasha's predicament and went online to buy a return ticket to Durham for a week on Saturday.

Sasha was horrified. 'You shouldn't have done that! You've made me feel so bad.'

Chloe stood firm. 'Not as bad as *we'd* feel if Grandpa Wilf found out the cost of train tickets these days.'

Kerstin nodded. 'What kind of a granddaughter would *you* be to spoil his excitement? Grandpa Wilf will be counting down the days until he sees you again. You can pay us back when you get a better job.'

Chloe winked. 'Or a rich man.'

*

Nine days later, Sasha climbed off the train in Durham to be met by her mother. 'Mum! It's so good to see you. Thanks for coming to pick me up. I'm sorry it's such a short visit, and I'm not staying overnight.'

Sasha's mum wasn't happy about that. 'You should have booked your return ticket for tomorrow. You know I have a hair appointment on Saturdays. I'll drop you at the care home and pick you up in time for you to catch the train back to London. Honestly, coming all this way just for lunch and a chat with my father isn't cost-effective at all.'

Sasha agreed with her mother, but she hadn't booked the tickets. Chloe and Kerstin were so kind and generous that she was just grateful to be here.

*

The care home had a large garden with manicured lawns and an abundance of flowers. Grandpa Wilf sat on a bench outside the main entrance, waiting for his granddaughter. As soon as he saw Sasha climb out of the car, he stood up to wave. Her mother sped off, and Sasha ran down the path to hug her grandfather. 'I'm so pleased to see you, Grandpa. This looks like a lovely place. Are you sure you're happy here?'

There was a twinkle in Grandpa Wilf's eyes. 'I can honestly say I've never been happier.' Sasha was surprised by that statement but thrilled by her grandfather's exuberance. She had to admit he had a spring in his step and more energy than the last time she'd seen him. 'Let's go to the cafeteria for lunch, and then I'll show you my new abode.'

Grandpa Wilf chose an egg mayonnaise baguette for lunch, and Sasha was shocked. 'Can you eat that with your teeth?'

'You sound like your mother. Angela's made me live off soup and bread for years; I've been deprived. Of course, I can eat a baguette. I cut it up with a knife to make it easier to bite and then enjoy every morsel. That's another thing; your mother didn't get me the best glue for my dentures. They have all the latest stuff here. I feel like a new man.'

Sasha laughed. 'Is Rupert in here having his lunch? I'd love to meet him.'

Grandpa Wilf's face clouded over. 'He's gone to a better place.'

Sasha's eyes widened. 'Oh, I'm so sorry about that. I did wonder why you were both in the same care home when Rupert obviously had more money. That house at the bottom of your garden was huge. Rupert will be having lobster for lunch at some posh boutique care home. I don't blame him. He should spend all his money while he can.'

Grandpa Wilf started choking on his baguette, and Sasha slapped his back before handing him a glass of water. 'Are you OK? You've gone a funny colour.'

'I'm fine, pet. Just a bit upset that the "better place" Rupert's gone to isn't on this earth.' Sasha gulped, and Grandpa Wilf continued, 'He left here in an ambulance two days ago. By the look of him, I'm certain he won't last the week. It comes to us all. That's why we need to make the most of every opportunity while we can. Now, let's change the subject. What would you like for dessert? I'm quite partial to a custard tart. Shall I get us a couple?'

A stroll around the gardens after lunch found Sasha in a reflective mood. She held her grandfather's arm and decided to visit him as often as possible. She had to keep swallowing hard to hold back the tears. When she returned to London, she would put all her energy into finding a new job. She needed more money so she could spend more time with her grandfather before it was too late. Rupert was here one minute and gone the next. Sasha stifled a sob as Grandpa Wilf unlocked the door to his apartment. It was cosy inside and had several photographs of her on the walls: her first day at school, her ballet solo, playing the piano at the Royal Albert Hall, and her Graduation Day.

Grandpa Wilf gestured to Sasha to sit at his small dining table before entering his bedroom and returning with a black sports bag. He sat opposite his granddaughter. 'As I said, we need to make the most of every opportunity while we can. With that in mind I want to give you your inheritance now.'

Sasha shook her head. 'You can't do that, Grandpa. Isn't it illegal? Don't you have to declare all your savings to the Government?'

Grandpa Wilf pushed the bag across the floor until it touched Sasha's feet. 'The money's all cash, pet. It's untraceable. Don't bank it. Spend it. And, most importantly, don't tell your mother about it.'

3

THE INHERITANCE

S asha sat on the train, reflecting on the afternoon's events. Her mother had queried why she was leaving the care home with a sports bag. Grandpa Wilf had been quick to answer. He told his daughter he wanted to donate some old clothes to the Battersea Dogs Home. Surprisingly, that reason was accepted without further questioning.

Sasha had already decided what she would spend her inheritance on. She would buy a train ticket once a month to return home to Durham. Grandpa Wilf had insisted she only return once a month as she should spend her weekends in London having the time of her life.

The sports bag was light, and Sasha envisaged an

old cereal box inside containing her grandfather's life savings in five and ten-pound notes. Grandpa Wilf always hid anything of importance in old cereal boxes. Her grandfather had never had a lot of money, and Sasha had gone along with being as thrilled as he was about the prospect of her now being a "woman of means". That's what he'd called her when he kissed her goodbye. She could still see him now, waving as her mother's car made its way down the rose-lined drive of Grandpa Wilf's "new abode".

Two hours into the three-hour journey, Sasha could no longer resist looking inside the sports bag. It was quiet in her carriage of the train, and when it stopped at a station, she reached up onto the overhead rack and pulled the bag onto the seat beside her. Her first sight as she opened the zip was of a handwritten note inside a clear plastic bag containing fifty-pound notes. It read: *One thousand.*

Sasha zipped the bag up and scanned the carriage around her. Her heart was thumping. There was more than one bag of money within the sports bag, and Sasha unzipped it again to establish there were ten bags of fifty-pound notes, all to the value of one thousand pounds! Grandpa Wilf had scrimped and scraped all his life to amass all this money for her? She knew she was special to him, but not this special! No wonder he didn't want her mother to find out.

Sasha threaded her arm through the handles of the bag. She couldn't believe she'd just left a fortune on an overhead rack without so much as a care. She'd even been down to the buffet carriage and bought a coffee while her inheritance had been left unattended. Now Sasha knew the amount; she felt uncomfortable walking through King's Cross Station alone. She messaged Chloe and Kerstin:

> *Hopefully one of you will see this in time. Please meet me at King's Cross at seven o'clock. I'll be outside the flower shop.*

Chloe responded straight away:

> *We're both together so will meet you at K.C. at 7. There's no need to buy us flowers, just pay us back for the train ticket when you come into some money lol. Anyway, RU OK? How's Grandpa Wilf?*

Sasha breathed a sigh of relief before messaging back:

> *I'm more than OK and Grandpa Wilf's never been better. See you soon!*

Chloe and Kerstin reached the flower shop before Sasha. They burst out laughing when they saw her walking along carrying a sports bag. Chloe hugged their friend before asking, 'Don't tell me Grandpa Wilf's been going to the gym, and he's talked you into doing the same?'

Sasha smiled. 'It's better than that. Sooo much better. Thanks for the suggestion about buying you both flowers. I'll pop into the shop and get you the biggest bunches I can find. Then we'll take a taxi home. I'm paying.' Chloe stared at Kerstin, who raised her eyebrows. Something major had happened in Durham, and they couldn't wait to find out what.

Sasha came out of the shop armed with flowers. The sports bag was still attached to her arm. 'Here you go, girls! Let's get to the taxi rank. Please walk either side of me. I can't lose this bag. Keep on the lookout for any dodgy characters.'

So, there it was. It was something to do with the sports bag. Grandpa Wilf probably had a valuable Ming vase or a Rolex he'd given to Sasha to get her through her cash crisis. Sasha had previously mentioned a cuckoo clock was his most valuable possession, and he'd promised to leave it to her in his Will.

Kerstin winked at Chloe before whispering, 'Cuckoo, cuckoo.'

Chloe winked in acknowledgement. The cuckoo clock was in the bag, and Sasha was going to sell it. Let's just hope they got it home in one piece.

Sasha was quiet in the taxi. However, she had a glow about her that her friends hadn't seen before. They sat either side of her in the back seat while she clung onto the sports bag. Their situation felt surreal, so the girls kept quiet, too. Sasha would no doubt update them on what happened in Durham when they reached the privacy of their apartment.

The taxi stopped, and Sasha pulled a fifty-pound note out of her purse to pay the driver – causing a jaw-dropping moment for her friends. It wasn't until they were inside their apartment with the door safely closed that Sasha lurched forward to hug her two best friends in the world. 'We're rich!'

Sasha bent down to unzip the sports bag to reveal the stash of money. Chloe and Kerstin were at a loss for words, so Sasha enlightened them, 'It's my inheritance. Grandpa Wilf has given it to me now so that he can see me enjoy it. I asked if that was illegal, but he said the money's untraceable, and I need to spend it. He wants to see me have a good time while he's still alive.' With her friends' eyes on stalks, Sasha said, 'There are only two conditions Grandpa Wilf stipulated before handing over the money: I shouldn't bank it, and I can't tell my mother.'

Kerstin's mouth had started working again, 'How much is there?'

'Ten thousand pounds, minus what I paid for your

flowers and the taxi. I'll be able to reimburse you for the train ticket now.'

Chloe didn't know whether to laugh or cry. She was sure something wasn't quite right about this, but she didn't want to dampen her friend's excitement. 'What about the cuckoo clock? You said that would be your "inheritance".'

'I know! Grandpa Wilf's kept that clock for years, even though it doesn't work. I've never even seen the cuckoo!'

Kerstin's head was spinning. 'You'll struggle to spend all that money without raising suspicion. Twenty-two-year-olds don't walk around London with fifty-pound notes in their bags.'

Sasha sighed. 'I did think of that. But then I had another thought.'

Chloe's eyes widened. 'What thought?'

'You two can help me. We'll spend a bit at a time; there's no need to rush. We can go into Oxford Street tomorrow and treat ourselves. That will be a start until I work out what to do with the rest. There must be a few people out there who would prefer to be paid in cash rather than by bank transfer. My mum always went to the bank to get cash to pay tradesmen who wanted to be paid "cash in hand".'

Chloe glanced at Kerstin. 'Sasha has a point.'

Sasha grinned. 'Stop worrying, you two. Grandpa Wilf has saved all his life for this day. You should have seen his face when he handed my inheritance over. He was so chuffed he had tears in his eyes. At least I can go to Durham to see him now. I've promised to go again next month.'

4

SPENDING SPREE

After sleeping on yesterday's surprising news, Chloe and Kerstin had come to terms with the endless possibilities Sasha's inheritance would bring her. They pushed any uneasy feelings away and joined in their friend's excitement. Today's first item on the agenda was to buy new clothes for Sasha. She'd no longer have just two blouses and one pair of trousers for work; she could turn up at the call centre in a different designer outfit every day.

Sasha emptied the contents of her makeup bag onto the kitchen table and asked her friends to do the same. She then opened three money bags and stuffed the makeup bags with fifty-pound notes. 'I'll feel safer walking around London if you both have some of the cash. No one would dream girls would go out in London with no makeup in their bags. I've thought of the perfect hiding place for a fortune.'

Sasha buried her makeup bag in the bottom of her canvas shopping bag and covered it with a scarf. She then hid the sports bag with the remaining money in the bottom of her wardrobe. At least, if the apartment were broken into, they'd have made a good start on spending the hard-earned money Grandpa Wilf had been saving all his life for his favourite granddaughter. It was such a shame he'd told Sasha not to bank it. Still, the worry of losing it was far outweighed by the excitement of spending it!

The first stop was Selfridges Beauty Hall, which smelt wonderful and had, until now, been way out of the girls' price range. New makeup and perfume for Sasha and her friends were a must. Embarrassed by the amount of money Sasha was spending on them, Chloe and Kerstin decided to go for a coffee instead of shopping for clothes. Sasha was in her element and skipped off to the clothes floor, gripping her canvas bag.

After a successful morning's shopping, it was time for lunch in an intimate bistro down a side street from the main shopping area. Chloe sighed as she looked around her. 'This place is so quaint and romantic. Look at that couple sitting next to the window and the two lovers at the table near the bar.'

Kerstin scoffed. 'How do you know they're

lovers?'

'He's playing footsie with her under the table.'

Kerstin bent down to look. 'So, he is. You should have been a detective.'

Sasha giggled. 'It's a shame we can't buy a set of boyfriends tailor-made to our requirements.'

Kerstin raised an eyebrow. 'Well, you probably could. You can buy anything in London.'

Chloe slapped Kerstin's arm. 'What are you like? Don't go giving Sasha ideas.'

Sasha sipped her wine. 'We won't need to buy boyfriends; we'll attract them after our makeovers.'

Chloe's head jerked around. 'What makeovers?'

'Well, while you two deserted me to go to a coffee shop earlier, I managed to get us all hair and makeup appointments for this afternoon. It's amazing what "cash upfront" can get you. People must think we're rich tourists.'

Chloe and Kerstin gave Sasha high fives before bursting into laughter. Kerstin grinned. 'Let's hope Sasha's right. We could have too many men to choose from by tonight.'

*

As the friends strolled out of the beauty salon, they could sense they were turning heads. Kerstin's short black hair perfectly framed her face, enhancing her bright green eyes. Chloe's strawberry blonde curls had been piled on her head and held in place with a silver satin ribbon, matching her light grey eyes. Sasha's long blonde hair fell in loose waves over her shoulders, and her blue eyes sparkled with mischievousness. They all looked great! Too good to spend a night in the apartment. Sasha was bursting with an idea, and she pushed open the door of an evening wear shop. Before her friends could protest, she instructed the sales assistant, 'Three evening dresses, please; we need them off the peg. There's no time for alterations. Can you help us?'

Sasha's dress was strapless, gold and shimmering. Chloe's was lilac and floaty, and Kerstin's was black and figure-hugging. All dresses were floor-length, and the only compromise they'd had to make was that Kerstin needed to wear flat shoes. Bags and shoes were all purchased to match. Happy with their choices, Sasha requested the labels be removed and their daywear be put into carrier bags.

When the girls left the shop this time, they really turned heads. Sasha flagged down a taxi. Chloe was in a daze. 'Where are we going?'

'To our apartment to drop off our shopping. Then to St Pancras.'

Kerstin gulped. 'Are we going on a train dressed like this?'

Sasha's heart pounded. 'No. There's just something I need to do.'

*

There are two public pianos in the main arcade of shops in St Pancras station. Two children were sitting at the first one, playing a duet. Sasha huffed and headed down the arcade to stand near the other one. Her embarrassed friends followed in hot pursuit. They didn't just look out of place in their glamorous dresses; they looked ridiculous rushing through a station's shopping arcade on a late Sunday afternoon, leaving heads turned in every direction.

An elderly gentleman sat at the second piano, playing a rendition of *The Blue Danube Waltz* by *Johann Strauss II*. Sasha loved that piece. She'd played it many times as a young girl. A shudder ran through her body; her father had been the one to take her to piano lessons twice a week from the age of five. Then, ten years later, when she'd played in a youth orchestra at the Royal Albert Hall, he'd been the one to come and watch her, along with Grandpa Wilf. That was the last time Sasha had played the piano. Her world collapsed soon after that when her parents split up.

A crowd had gathered, and when the music

stopped, the pianist stood up to take a bow. Sasha edged forward to stand next to the piano. There were whistles and shouts of 'Encore!' and the man sat down to play the piece again. Sasha's shoulders slumped. She'd been brave enough to come here to see if she could still play the piano, but she was quickly losing her nerve. She knew her friends weren't happy about being the centre of attention to appease her impulsive whim. The crowd was now clapping in time to the music, and Sasha turned around to see her friends waltzing with two men in dinner suits. Her mouth fell open.

Sasha then noticed a man bowing down in front of her. He wasn't moving. She poked him on his shoulder. The man stood to face her. 'Lawrie! What are you doing here?'

Lawrie flashed his trademark cheeky grin. 'May I have this dance?'

Sasha stamped her foot. 'No!'

Lawrie frowned. 'But I'm your boss, remember. You can surely stop me from looking like a fool in front of this crowd. I was bowing down for ages before you noticed me.'

Sasha snorted and flung a hand to her mouth before responding with a straight face, 'There's not enough time for a dance now. The piece is nearly finished.'

Lawrie nodded over his shoulder. 'That's no excuse. My friends will do the right thing and command another encore. Mikey's whistle can stop trains. Trust me, the pianist will be sitting back down before he can take a bow.'

Sasha threw a hand to her mouth again when she saw another two young men in dinner suits standing behind her boss. She guessed the two dancing with her friends were part of the same group who all looked just as out of place as *they* did. Sasha turned to face Lawrie; she had to admit he looked suave wearing a bow tie. 'Why are you all here dressed as penguins?'

Lawrie laughed. 'We're off to the champagne bar before we go to the casino. May I ask why you're all here dressed as goddesses?'

Before Sasha could think of a reason, there was a piercing whistle and more chants of 'Encore!'. She looked over at Chloe and Kerstin, who were flushed with excitement. Sasha held out her right hand, and Lawrie took hold of it while sliding an arm around her waist. Before long, he was twirling the golden goddess around the shopping arcade at St Pancras station.

5

CHAMPAGNE BAR

The girls no longer felt out of place; they were now sitting in the champagne bar in their evening dresses with five handsome men wearing dinner suits. Sasha had been right; their makeovers had worked wonders, and as Kerstin had hoped, they now had too many men to choose from.

Lawrie and Mikey were chatting to Chloe. And Kerstin only had eyes for tall, dark-haired Adam – her dancing partner from earlier. That left Sasha with Rafferty and Oswald. It soon became apparent all five had been travelling companions during their gap year. Sasha's eyes were glued to Oswald's phone as he scrolled through an album of photographs of their exploits. Bali was a highlight when Rafferty proposed to Oswald on the beach, and Adam seemed to attract every tall blonde model in sight.

Sasha couldn't help but comment, 'There aren't many photographs of Lawrie and Mikey. Are they too risqué to show me?'

Oswald's face clouded over. 'Mikey's father became ill three weeks into our travels. Mikey and Lawrie returned to the UK to be with him until the end. Those two have been best friends since they were seven. We decided to meet up this weekend to boost Mikey's spirits. Probably best you don't mention his dad.'

Tears welled up in Sasha's eyes. 'That's so sad. I promise not to mention anything. Why don't we all come to the casino with you? Mikey seems to be getting along well with Chloe. He wasn't dancing with her earlier, though, was he?'

Oswald put his hand up. 'That was me. If there's one fault I can find with Rafferty, it's that he doesn't like to shine in public until he's had a few cocktails.'

Rafferty held his champagne glass in the air. 'Too right! Anyway, Sasha, why were you trying to muscle in on that gentleman playing the piano? You tried to push him off the stool with your eyes – I saw you.'

Sasha blushed. 'I wanted to have a go. I played the piano when I was younger.'

Oswald stood up and offered his arm to Sasha. 'Please allow me to escort you. The piano's available now – you can live your dream.'

Sasha gulped. She looked at the others and was relieved to see they were all in deep conversation. It wouldn't hurt if she had a quick go. It would satisfy her urge if nothing else. She linked her arm through Oswald's and held her breath as he guided her to the "stage". Sasha sat down, and Oswald adjusted her dress over the stool. 'Don't start until I'm ready. I want to film this.' Sasha's fingers touched the keys, and she began to play.

As before, a crowd began to gather. Rafferty alerted Chloe and Kerstin, 'Sasha's performing.' Lawrie jumped out of his seat, and Mikey followed. Adam and Rafferty chose to stay behind to look after the jackets, bags and drinks. Rafferty offered Adam a peanut. 'Oswald will be filming this. You know what he's like with social media. We'll get a video within minutes of Sasha's performance ending.'

Chloe held her hand to her heart as she linked arms with Kerstin. 'Sasha mentioned she'd played the piano when she was younger. She didn't say how good she was!'

Kerstin's eyes widened. 'She's wasted at that call centre. Now we know why she brought us here all dressed up to the nines. Our friend is a dark horse,'

Kerstin turned to wink at Chloe, 'and we wouldn't want her any other way.'

There was no need for Mikey's loud whistle and shouts of 'Encore!' Sasha was in a world of her own and played six classical pieces in a row. The audience listened in awe to the brilliant pianist in her gold shimmery evening gown. Sasha was a sight to behold, and when she'd played her final note, she stood up and walked back to the champagne bar without acknowledging the crowd's rapture.

Oswald was devastated. He chased after her. 'I had such a good piece of film, and you spoilt it at the end. That dress is perfect for curtseying. You just walked off like you were in a trance.'

Sasha's heart was pounding. She hadn't felt so alive in years. Whatever Oswald was going on about went in one ear and out the other. Oswald showed Rafferty the film's ending, and his fiancé slapped him on the back. 'That's brilliant! Sasha looks like an angel who's come down from heaven and is now on her way back. We know she's back at the champagne bar, but others don't need to know that. She looks surreal; that could be her USP.'

Oswald's eyes widened. 'Her Unique Selling Point! You are so right, Rafferty.'

Sasha drank her champagne and tried to change

the subject from her piano-playing skills. 'I no longer want to hear about that embarrassing moment. It was just something I needed to do after seeing a photograph of me playing the piano on the wall of my grandfather's care home yesterday. I'd blanked that part of my life from my memory, and it needs to go back into its box. Now, let's go to the casino.'

Lawrie's mouth fell open. 'You're coming to the casino?'

Sasha nodded. 'We certainly are. Lead the way.'

Oswald gulped. He'd already pinged off the video to his vast range of followers. Sasha shouldn't be hiding her light under a bushel. It wasn't his fault he was quick off the mark and keen to promote his friend's talent. Sasha was a friend of Lawrie's, but any friend of Lawrie's was a friend of his. He put his phone in his pocket and decided to deal with all the messages sliding through in the morning – when Sasha was far enough away not to complain.

Chloe and Kerstin wouldn't let Sasha hear the end of this. They'd interrogate her tomorrow if she didn't want to talk now. She had a gift she'd been hiding all these years, and they wanted to know why. In the meantime, Mikey and Adam escorted them both to a taxi and gave instructions to the driver. The girls saw Sasha standing on the pavement as their taxi sped off. Sasha had no choice but to jump into a taxi with the others.

Chloe felt quite excited; she'd never been to a casino. Kerstin was more interested in Adam's long black hair and blue eyes. The saying "tall, dark and handsome" didn't do justice to the man now squeezing her hand in the back of a taxi on the way to a casino in the heart of London. Sasha's impromptu "spending spree" had worked wonders.

Sasha sat wedged between Oswald and Rafferty and opposite Lawrie in the back of their taxi. She was annoyed about Chloe and Kerstin. They'd deserted her at a mere whiff of eligible men. Well, tonight, Sasha was on her own, and she would try her best to push herself out of her comfort zone. She had six hundred pounds in her evening bag, all in fifty-pound notes. If her friends hadn't left her on the pavement at St. Pancras looking like a lemon, she would have split the money between the three of them at the casino. Well, ha-ha, not now. Sasha was going to gamble like the boys.

6

THE CASINO

Lawrie was surprised to see Sasha pay for her casino chips with fifty-pound notes. Something didn't add up. He'd only been working with her for two weeks at the call centre, but during that time, he'd come under the impression she was strapped for cash. Was she leading two lives? Adam, the most experienced gambler out of the group of friends, had now diverted his attention from Kerstin to Sasha. Lawrie wasn't surprised; Adam preferred blondes.

Kerstin stood next to Chloe with a frown on her face. 'Sasha's being so selfish. She's throwing money around like she's some rich person.'

Chloe stared at Kerstin. 'It's not just the money. You're jealous Adam's taken her under his wing.'

Kerstin shrugged her shoulders. 'I'm not bothered. Adam will lose interest in her when her money's run out.' Kerstin checked her watch. 'I'll give Sasha half an hour to lose a fortune; she's so naïve. People don't win in these places. I'd rather spend my money on a drink. Mikey's deserted you, too. Let's go to the bar and drown our sorrows.'

Sasha was grateful for Adam's advice. She was enjoying the excitement of learning something new. This could be an easy way to shift all those fifty-pound notes and make a profit in the process! Adam said any winnings could be transferred directly into Sasha's bank account. That took a weight off her shoulders; she'd much rather have her inheritance in the bank than at the bottom of her wardrobe. It was a pity she'd only brought six hundred pounds with her tonight.

Two hours later, Sasha decided to call it a day. It was ten o'clock, and tomorrow was Monday. That meant an early start to get to the call centre. She searched for Lawrie, who, unknown to her, had been watching her all evening. She turned and met his concerned gaze. 'Are you OK, Sasha?'

Sasha nodded. 'It's been a good experience. I'm heading off now. We need to be up early in the morning for work. Do you know where the girls are?'

'They're up at the bar with a few admirers.'

Sasha frowned and went in search of her friends, who were laughing and joking with a group of men.

She waved an arm in the air. 'Chloe! Kerstin! We should head off home now. It's ten o'clock.'

Kerstin waved an arm back. 'You go. We're having too much fun to leave now. The evening's only just beginning. Don't wait up for us.'

Lawrie noticed Sasha's face drop, and he searched for Mikey. 'Make sure Chloe and Kerstin don't get into trouble with those men over there. I'm going to take Sasha home. Tell the guys I'll be in touch tomorrow.'

Sasha couldn't be more disappointed with her friends. First, they'd left her on the pavement at St Pancras, and then they'd been more than happy to let her take a taxi home alone. If Sasha hadn't paid for their makeovers and bought them those dresses, they wouldn't be sitting at a bar now in a plush casino having the time of their lives. Sasha held her head high. At times like this, she knew who her friends were.

Sasha pushed open the casino door to see Lawrie standing beside a taxi. 'Your carriage awaits, Cinderella. Let's get you home before it turns into a pumpkin and I turn into a rat or something. Normality will return in the morning, and we'll both be back in the call centre trying to impress my mother. Tonight will seem like a lifetime ago.'

Sasha climbed into the back of the taxi, and Lawrie climbed in after her. She took hold of his hand and squeezed it. 'Thanks for looking out for me. It means a lot. I enjoyed this evening, I think! I can't believe what I did at St Pancras; I was in a daze. I did do that, didn't I?'

Lawrie could see the taxi driver's eyes widen in his rearview mirror. 'Yes, you did do it. I'm sure it'll be on the main news headlines tomorrow.' The taxi driver blushed; the girl in the back was probably a streaker.

Sasha slapped Lawrie's arm. 'Don't worry me. I only did it to get rid of an urge that was brought to the forefront of my mind after visiting my grandfather yesterday in his care home. That's all there was to it.' The taxi driver raised his eyebrows as he pulled up outside Sasha's apartment.

Lawrie insisted on paying the fare. 'I'll jump out, too. I can walk home from here.'

The taxi sped off, leaving Sasha and Lawrie standing on the pavement. Sasha smiled at her boss before questioning him, 'Why didn't you tell your mother you weren't travelling the world during your gap year?'

Lawrie blushed. 'Who told you?'

'Oswald. He showed me photographs of your gap year on his phone, and I noticed you weren't in many of them. I also know about Mikey's dad. Why doesn't your mother know what you were up to?'

Lawrie sighed. 'Because she never pays attention to me. I tell her things, and she doesn't listen. She wasn't interested in what I was doing during my gap year. All she's bothered about is her call centre. She doesn't know what I want to do with my life.'

'What do you want to do with your life?'

'Run a farm.'

'A farm?'

'That's right – Mikey's dad's farm. I spent a lot of time helping when I was younger. I was on the farm more than at home in London. That suited my mother so she could build her business empire.'

'I wouldn't say the call centre was a "business empire".'

'Exactly. But my mother thinks it is. It's her life. It's taught me one good thing, though.'

'What's that?'

'Family is more important than a successful career.'

Sasha smiled. 'You can have both if you get the balance right.'

Lawrie thrust his hands in his pockets and shuffled his feet. 'I should head off now. You wanted an early night. Congratulations on your win, by the way. I had goosebumps watching you make those daredevil moves.'

Sasha blushed. 'It all came down to Adam's help *and* a great deal of luck.'

'Night, Sasha. See you at work in the morning.'

'Night, Lawrie.'

7

MONDAY MORNING

Sasha jumped into the shower. She was feeling bright and refreshed and looking forward to going to work in one of her new outfits. She took time to do her hair and makeup and squirted on her new perfume. When she entered the kitchen, she could see no sign of Chloe and Kerstin, who were usually up and ready before her. Her stomach sank. Had they come home last night? Sasha knocked on their bedroom doors. Thankfully, they were both worse for wear and sleeping in rather than having been abducted.

Sasha tutted. Phoning in to work sick on a Monday morning was a telltale sign of a raucous weekend. Still, her friends had got themselves into this state. She'd tried to drag them away from the casino at a respectable time. Sasha had no time to worry about them. She was concerned, though, and that was for

Lawrie. She didn't know if she could look his mother in the eye today without giving her the evils. Margaret was such a selfish person. Sasha sighed; her own mother was selfish, too. Were all mothers selfish? At least she could relate to Lawrie and wanted to learn more about the farm. Was Lawrie thinking about running it with Mikey?

Word had spread around the call centre about Sasha's performance at St Pancras. Oswald's video was all over the internet. The grapevine had started yesterday evening, and when Sasha walked into the office, she was met by a sea of smiling faces. Margaret was in her office, and the team had to "behave" while she was in earshot. Sasha noticed a few thumbs-up signs, winks, and someone pretending to play the piano on his desk.

Noticing Sasha's confusion, one of the girls brought the video up on her phone and placed it on Sasha's desk with the sound off. The girl scribbled a note and showed it to Sasha.

> *You're a superstar! The whole team's in awe of you x*

Lawrie bounded into the office with a bouquet. 'This has just arrived for Sasha. I picked it up on the way in.' Sasha opened the handwritten envelope and removed the card. It read:

> *Thanks for the chat. L x*

Sasha smiled as she held Lawrie's gaze. Lawrie was pleased the change in Sasha had continued from yesterday. She glowed, and she looked much better in a different work outfit. Those old blouses hadn't done her justice. A blue dress brought out the colour of her eyes.

By lunchtime, Sasha had received three bouquets. The second one to arrive was from Oswald with a message:

> *You're mega-trending Darling!*
>
> *Don't be cross with me. The world loves you. Oswald X*

The third bouquet was from Chloe and Kerstin:

> *Thank you for our treats. We had a great weekend. Sorry we're rubbish friends. Dinner's on us tonight! C&K xx*

Sasha carried the third bouquet into the ladies' cloakroom. She'd filled one of the hand basins with water and propped the latest flowers against the others. When she stepped back into the corridor, Lawrie was waiting for her. Sasha blushed. 'There was no need to buy me flowers.'

Lawrie laughed. 'So, I gather. Who sent the other ones?'

'Oswald and my so-called friends.'

Lawrie smiled. 'Don't be too hard on them. They

were only keeping themselves entertained while you hijacked Adam for his gambling expertise.'

Sasha sighed. 'I hadn't thought of it like that. Kerstin was keen on Adam. She would have been livid with me.'

'Well, the grapevine tells me she won't be livid with you anymore.'

'What grapevine?'

'Oswald. He's always good for passing on gossip.'

Sasha giggled. 'Tell me more.'

The couple were rudely interrupted by Margaret approaching with her eyes narrowed. 'You two can get back to your desks right away. I'm most annoyed with you, Lawrence. You should be setting an example as team leader. I'm not paying you both to stand around chatting in the corridor.'

Margaret marched off, and Lawrie called after her, 'You're not paying me for working here. I'll be taking a long lunch today with Sasha.'

Margaret carried on marching, and Lawrie turned to Sasha. 'See? She never listens to me.'

Sasha's face dropped. 'I can't take a long lunch. I'll get fired.'

Lawrie grinned. 'I have an idea. Let's both get fired. Pack your things, bring the flowers, and we'll take the afternoon off while we decide what to do with the rest of our lives.'

Sasha spluttered, 'But I need this job to pay my share of the rent on the apartment.'

Lawrie winked. 'Don't forget your winnings from last night. Four thousand pounds will tide you over while you get on the right career path.'

Sasha's heart leapt. Four thousand plus seven thousand in the sports bag would take the pressure off for a while. Any guilt she'd felt about splashing three thousand pounds in a day on makeovers for her and the girls had been washed away when the roulette wheel stopped, and the winning number was *Red Twenty-Seven*. Even Adam had been nervous when she decided to go for that final bet. What a weekend it had been! First, her inheritance, then her win at the casino. Her luck was in!

Sasha smiled at Lawrie. 'I have a better idea. We should both resign. Let's type up our resignations and tape them to our screens. When your mother comes looking for us, she'll see them straight away.'

Lawrie gave Sasha a high five. 'Deal! I'll meet you back here in fifteen minutes. I'll help you carry the flowers.'

8

ALL'S NOT AS IT SEEMS

Sitting in a pub garden overlooking the Thames was a much more pleasurable experience than working in a call centre on a sunny Monday afternoon. Lawrie was a considerate companion. He'd held Sasha's chair out for her to sit down and popped into the bar to request a bucket of water for her flowers. He was concerned they would wilt in the heat. The flowers were now in the bucket in the shade underneath their table.

Sasha clinked her wine glass against Lawrie's beer glass. 'You go first. How are we going to turn you into a farmer?'

Lawrie sipped his beer and then leaned back in his chair. 'I'm well on the way down my chosen path. Mikey and I just need to draw up some contracts.

We're going to run the farm together. It'll be a hoot. I've got the brains, and Mikey's got the brawn.'

Sasha laughed. 'From what I've seen of Mikey, he's brainy too. He knows a good woman when he sees one – he's got a soft spot for Chloe.'

Lawrie put his glass down before rubbing his hands together. 'That reminds me. I didn't finish telling you about Adam and Kerstin.'

Sasha leaned forward on the table. 'Go on. Don't keep me in suspense.'

'After we left the casino, Adam walked over to the bar, planted a smacker on Kerstin's lips and whisked her away to a nightclub.'

'What?! In front of that group of men?'

'That's what Oswald says. Trust Adam to behave like James Bond. Sounds like Kerstin approved. She must have done if he spent the night at yours.'

Sasha gulped. 'He was in her room when I knocked this morning?'

'Apparently so. I thought Adam preferred blondes; Kerstin isn't his usual type.'

'Was Mikey in Chloe's room?'

'No. He doesn't kiss on the first date.'

Sasha was shocked. 'You know more about what's going on in my apartment than I do.'

Lawrie lowered his eyes. 'I know about the sports bag too. Kerstin mentioned it to Adam. We're all concerned about your inheritance. There's something not right about your grandfather having all those fifty-pound notes batched up and hidden.'

A shudder ran through Sasha. 'Kerstin shouldn't have mentioned the money. Just wait until I see her! And … and … my inheritance is none of your business. How can you question my grandfather's integrity? Grandpa Wilf is as honest as they come.' Sasha's phone rang, and she looked daggers at Lawrie. 'That's him now. Grandpa calls me at lunchtime when he wants to chat.' Sasha took the call, 'Hello, Grandpa. How's the weather in Durham today? It's lovely and sunny here in London.'

Grandpa Wilf wasn't his usual cheery self. 'I've had some bad news about Rupert.'

Sasha held a hand to her heart. 'Oh, Grandpa. I'm so sorry for your loss. If there's one consolation, you were expecting it and Rupert's finally gone to a better place.'

Grandpa Wilf sounded agitated, 'You don't understand, Sasha. He's back here in the next apartment.'

Sasha's heart sank. Something was wrong. Her grandfather only called her "Sasha" when she was in trouble. She much preferred him calling her "pet". 'Have I done something wrong?'

'Yes! You're all over the internet.'

Sasha cringed. 'You've seen that in the care home?'

Grandpa Wilf sighed. 'No. Rupert's grandson's into all that social media stuff, and he recognised you.'

'Recognised me?'

'Yes. On the CCTV of this place. He saw you walking out carrying the sports bag. He knows you're my granddaughter – he's seen photos of you on my wall. If you hadn't been seen in St Pancras last night, he'd be none the wiser about where you lived.'

Sasha rubbed her forehead. 'Does the sports bag belong to Rupert?'

'No. It's Blake's.'

'Who's Blake?'

'Rupert's grandson.'

Sasha's head was spinning. She felt sick, faint, and embarrassed all rolled into one. Lawrie reached across the table to squeeze her hand. He had been right to be worried for her. The money wasn't Grandpa Wilf's – it was Blake's.

Grandpa Wilf coughed before continuing, 'Anyway, I've given Blake your address, and he's coming down to London with your inheritance in return for his bag.'

'My inheritance?'

'Yes, the cuckoo clock. You can have it early. I must go now, Sasha, or I'll be late for lunch. It's shepherd's pie today.'

Sasha dropped her phone on the table and held her head in her hands. 'I can't believe it. Grandpa Wilf lied to me. What am I going to do?' Sasha didn't wait for an answer. She *had* to get three thousand pounds of last night's winnings into the sports bag without delay. She stared at Lawrie. 'Do you think the winnings will be in my bank account yet?'

Lawrie rubbed his forehead. 'They could take a couple of days to clear. Besides, you'll need to give notice if you want to draw out such a large sum. I'm not an expert on money laundering. I'm just guessing the bank will have restrictions for what you can do at the drop of a hat.'

'Money laundering! You make it sound like I'm a drug dealer or something.'

The couple locked eyes – was Blake a drug dealer?! If so, Sasha was in serious trouble. Lawrie reached for his phone and handed Sasha's to her. 'Contact Chloe and Kerstin, and I'll message the boys. If we all withdraw cash from our banks this afternoon, we should be able to make up the three thousand. Adam will be good for at least a grand. He's always got ready cash. You can return the money to everyone when your winnings come through.'

Sasha nodded. There was no time to waste. It was only a three-hour train journey from Durham to London. She blocked the thought that Blake may get here sooner by private jet. It depended on how big a drug dealer he was. The other thought was that armed bodyguards may accompany him. Now Sasha felt sick. She tried to block that thought, too.

It was easy for Chloe and Kerstin to get to their banks as they had the day off work. Lawrie managed the logistics of collecting cash from his friends, who were all in different parts of London. The only one missing was Mikey, who'd driven back to the farm this morning.

By four o'clock, Lawrie was counting the cash in Sasha's apartment. Chloe and Kerstin had recovered from their hangovers and were now angry at Sasha's latest news – how could her grandfather put her at risk by involving her in a drug gang?

Sasha sat on the sofa, cradling a mug of hot, sweet tea. Chloe had said it was good for shock. Sasha's head was spinning. Once she'd paid everyone back for their loans, she would only have a thousand pounds left, and her rent would soon eat away at that. She should never have taped her resignation to her screen this morning. First thing tomorrow, she'd need to find another job. Any job.

Lawrie sighed. 'We're two hundred short. I've just messaged Mikey, and he's on his way back from the farm. He'll be here in forty minutes.'

The intercom sounded, and Chloe answered it. Everyone looked at her with their eyes on stalks. Why did she do that? They weren't prepared yet to meet with a criminal. For one thing, they didn't have all his money. It was too late – a man's voice sounded through the speaker:

Hi, my name's Blake, and I've come to see Sasha.

Chloe thought he sounded quite nice. There was no need to remain in this state of fear for a moment longer. Blake would understand they'd temporarily borrowed some of his money. Waiting another forty minutes for two hundred pounds shouldn't be a problem. Chloe decided to take control:

Come on up.

Kerstin pushed Chloe into her bedroom. 'We'll need to hide. He won't want us to know about his stash of cash. Lawrie should hide with us, too.'

Lawrie was uncomfortable about that, but he could see Kerstin's point. 'We'll only be in the next room, Sasha. We'll be listening, and if there's any sign of trouble, I'll be straight out to rescue you.'

9

THE SPORTS BAG

Sasha opened the door to the sight of a giant of a man wearing a rugby shirt and jeans. He had unruly brown hair and piercing blue eyes. He held his hand out, and Sasha took hold of it. His handshake was surprisingly warm and soft. In his left hand, he was carrying a shopping bag with the top of Grandpa Wilf's cuckoo clock peeping out of it. He didn't look like a drug dealer.

Sasha gestured for him to sit down. 'Would you like a cup of tea?'

Blake flashed a dimpled smile. 'That would be great if it's not too much trouble. I had one on the train, but it's not the same as one made in a teapot.'

Sasha looked down at the teapot in her hands. 'I know what you mean. I find that coffee usually tastes better than tea on the train. There's not much in it, though.'

Blake laughed as he held out the shopping bag. 'Anyway, the reason I'm here is to do a swap-over. Your grandfather thought he'd put the clock in my sports bag, and that's why he gave it to you. What I'm trying to understand is how he got hold of my sports bag in the first place. I'd left it in *my* grandfather's apartment. Still, dementia is a terrible thing. It's impossible to have a sensible conversation with either Wilf or Rupert.'

Sasha gulped – Grandpa Wilf didn't have dementia, far from it. 'I heard you'd checked the CCTV and saw me leaving with the bag. I feel like a criminal. Grandpa told me it was my inheritance. I didn't look inside the bag until I was nearly home on the train.'

Blake sipped his tea. 'It didn't take me long to put two and two together. You were fresh in my mind from your performance at St Pancras last night. My mate, Adam, forwarded the video to our rugby team. He's been boasting about knowing you. Then, when I popped in to say "hi" to Wilf, the photo of you playing the piano on his wall caught my eye.' Blake chuckled. 'I bet you were surprised to find a rugby kit in the bag instead of a cuckoo clock.'

Chloe's mouth fell open, Lawrie raised his eyebrows, and Kerstin sprang into action. The sports bag was on the floor in Chloe's bedroom. She tipped it upside down and pushed the cash under Chloe's bed. Lawrie and Chloe were rigid with shock. Kerstin then zipped up the bag and walked into the living room. 'You must be Blake. Adam's told me all about you. What a small world this is.'

Kerstin handed the bag to Blake. 'I have a confession to make before you open it.' Blake frowned, and Kerstin continued, 'We had no idea why Sasha's grandfather had sent her back to London with a rugby kit and, as there was a charity bag due for collection yesterday, I got rid of it.'

Blake gasped. 'You got rid of my rugby kit?'

Kerstin gave her best smile. 'Well, if I'd known it belonged to you, my boyfriend could have returned it.'

'Who's your boyfriend?'

'Your "mate" Adam. Now, as a gesture of goodwill on my part, I'll pay for a replacement kit. Just let me know the cost.'

It was Blake's turn to be in shock. 'There's no need for that. I'll say my kit shrank in the wash. I'll pick up another one from the club.' Blake eyed Kerstin up and down. 'Wow! Adam's done well moving on from blondes. I never thought he'd make the shift.'

Kerstin blushed while maintaining eye contact with Blake, who seemed in no hurry to leave. He was on his third cup of tea when Kerstin saw Mikey's car pull into the car park. She removed the plate of biscuits Sasha had put on the coffee table and smiled at their visitor. 'We don't mean to be rude, but we have another appointment soon. Thank you for ensuring Sasha's inheritance arrived safely.'

Mikey strode through the car park as Blake strolled out of the apartment building. He buzzed on the intercom. 'I'm here. I've got the cash.'

Lawrie released the lock for Mikey to enter. The girls were all huddled on the sofa in a state of trauma, and Mikey stared at his friend. 'Am I too late? Has the drug dealer been in touch?'

Lawrie shook his head. 'There's no drug dealer. The guy's in the same rugby team as Adam. I recognised him when I looked out of the window just now.'

Kerstin threw a hand to her chest. She'd winged it by taking Blake's story as the truth. Her thoughts turned to Adam in a rugby kit, and a smile lit up her face. Chloe shuddered at the sight of Kerstin's glazed eyes and rushed to make her a strong, sweet cup of tea. Her hands were shaking; this was all too much to take in.

Lawrie updated Mikey and then called Adam. Blake's story checked out. He was born in Durham and now lives in London. Blake had taken his kit to Durham to wear on a stag do. He'd left the sports bag for his grandfather to look after while he flew to Barcelona for a week on business. That news led to the obvious question – how did the money get into the sports bag?

Sasha's shock turned to anger, and she paced around the kitchen. 'My grandfather knew there was money in the bag. How could I have been so stupid to think it was his life's savings? If Blake left the bag with his sports kit with his grandfather a week ago, then Rupert must have swapped the kit for the cash before he was taken to the hospital. Grandpa Wilf thought his friend was on his deathbed, and he jumped at the chance to steal from him. I will never forgive him!'

Sasha sat on the sofa and wrung her hands in her lap to stop them from trembling. 'Thank you all so much for lending me your cash. You can take it back now.'

Kerstin had drunk enough sweet tea. She headed for the fridge and opened a bottle of wine. 'Anyone for a tipple while we decide what to do with the seven thousand pounds under Chloe's bed?'

Chloe gasped. 'It's Sasha's money, not ours.'

Sasha shook her head. 'It's not my money. I want nothing to do with it. My rightful inheritance arrived this afternoon in the form of a cuckoo clock. Besides, when I can access my winnings, I'll be returning the three thousand I spent.'

Kerstin handed beers to Lawrie and Mikey before staring at Sasha. 'Who will you be returning the money to? Rupert's in no fit state to come looking for it. Besides, we don't know if he hid the money in the bag – that's an assumption on your part. We should keep quiet until things calm down.'

Sasha reached for her phone. 'I'll get to the bottom of it. I'm calling Grandpa Wilf.'

The friends held their breath to hear what Grandpa Wilf had to say, 'Blake didn't ask how I got hold of the bag, did he?'

'No. He thinks you've got dementia. He said he can't have a sensible conversation with you.'

'Good. Good. Well done for handing the bag back, Sasha. That's a weight lifted from my shoulders. I must go now. Rupert passed away half an hour ago. I'm joining the other residents in the social lounge for a little tipple of rum as a mark of respect.'

Sasha threw her phone on the sofa. She was so annoyed with her grandfather. He'd left her with an enormous problem by refusing to tell her the truth about the money. It blatantly wasn't his to give to her. She raised her arms in the air. 'What are we going to do?'

Kerstin sipped her wine. 'We do nothing. If the money had a connection to Rupert, then it's now become well and truly adrift.'

Chloe gulped. 'Poor Blake. He'll be heading up to Durham next time for a funeral. A stag do, then a funeral in such a short space of time. I wonder if anyone he knows up there is pregnant? At least a christening will be nicer than a funeral. They say these things go in threes.'

Kerstin narrowed her eyes. What on earth was Chloe rambling on about? The friends were all in a difficult situation. Someone needed to take control before it got out of hand. Kerstin was best placed to take charge in a crisis; she'd been head girl at school. She directed her gaze at Lawrie and Mikey. 'You're welcome to join us for dinner tonight. Chloe and I are treating Sasha. Feel free to bring your friends along – we can hand their money back and make sure we're all joined together in a circle of trust while we get to the bottom of this.'

Sasha was calming down. She thought back to Grandpa Wilf's words on Saturday:

We need to make the most of every opportunity while we can.

Her grandfather had undoubtedly made the most of an opportunity, even though he wouldn't admit it. Sasha's guilt was eased by viewing her brief inheritance as a loan. If she hadn't spent three thousand pounds, she wouldn't have been at the casino to win four. Also, playing the piano at St Pancras station would have remained a dream forever.

10

THE CIRCLE OF TRUST

Adam chewed on his sirloin steak as he pondered the chain of events that had led him to Kerstin. She was taking control of a bizarre situation, and the group of friends were hanging onto her every word. Dark-haired, passionate Kerstin was different from the blonde supermodels he usually went for. She had depth and ideas that even *he* wouldn't have thought of. He spared a thought for Blake, who had just lost his grandfather *and* his rugby kit. Kerstin's quick thinking this afternoon had severed all links between the money and the care home. Adam was proud of his new girlfriend. She'd told Blake that's who she was, and Adam didn't mind at all.

Kerstin kept her voice low as she scanned the faces around the table, 'So, are we all in agreement then? We'll keep the secret between us for now. There's no need for Grandpa Wilf to spend his remaining years behind bars, and Blake can remember his grandfather without the knowledge that he may have been doing dodgy dealings. We can't prove that was the case, so why blot Rupert's memory?' The friends all clinked glasses in an unspoken confirmation of their pact.

Oswald was keen to change the subject to less stressful things and directed his attention to Sasha, 'What are we going to do with you, my darling? How are we going to turn you into a superstar? Rafferty and I have been speaking, and we could give you a "leg up", so to speak, onto the global stage.'

Rafferty nodded. 'That's right. Our friend, Paulo, is the head concierge at the Wensley International in the West End. There's a grand piano on the mezzanine floor above the reception. We've never heard anyone playing it. Paulo says it's just there for show and that it was a stupid idea to put it up there when it would have been better placed in the bar. Still, Paulo says the hotel owner insisted the piano was placed there so that he could see it whenever he walked into the foyer.'

Oswald rubbed his hands together. 'So, we've had an idea. Why don't you pop along and have a little play? I could film you; it would be the second instalment of "The Angel from Heaven". You'll just need to get up and walk away again in a trance like you did at St

Pancras.'

Sasha blushed. 'You're kidding me. What would the hotel owner say?'

Oswald smiled. 'He won't know, darling, he's never there. Paulo hasn't seen him for years.'

Sasha sighed. 'I don't know. I've got the urge to play the piano out of my system. I need to focus on finding a job. It wasn't the best idea of mine this morning for Lawrie and me to tape our resignations to our screens and leave Margaret in the lurch.'

Lawrie reached into his pocket and took out two crumpled notes. 'Talking of that, I have a confession to make. I thought you were being too reckless, so I grabbed our resignations and popped into my mother's office to advise her you weren't feeling well and that I was taking you home. So, I'm the only one in trouble for taking the rest of the afternoon off.'

Sasha leaned forward and kissed Lawrie on his cheek. 'You're a lifesaver! I've had a whirlwind of a few days. I need time to sit back and take stock of my life. At least, thanks to you, I'm not under pressure to find a job while I come to terms with losing my grandfather.'

Chloe gasped. 'Grandpa Wilf's not died as well, has he?'

Sasha finished chewing a mouthful of pasta before she responded, 'No, I'm disowning him. How could he lie to me *and* stop calling me "pet"? He's not the man I thought he was.'

Kerstin whispered to Chloe, 'She doesn't mean it.'

Sasha wiped her mouth on a serviette before turning to Lawrie again. 'Before we were rudely interrupted at lunchtime by my ex-grandfather, you were going to tell me more about your dreams of becoming a farmer.'

Chloe and Kerstin's ears pricked up, and Lawrie smiled at Mikey, who took the lead in divulging their plans. 'The guys all know about this, but for the sake of Chloe, Kerstin and Sasha, I'll give you some insight into our plans. My father passed away a few months ago and left the family farm to me. Lawrie has helped on the farm during school holidays since we were young, so it's no surprise he's agreed to go into partnership with me to make the farm the hub of the community in our village.'

Sasha smiled at Lawrie. 'Are you bringing any bright ideas to the project?'

Lawrie touched his cheek. Did Sasha really kiss him? That was a turn-up for the books! He smiled back at her while locking eyes with this woman who had only been in his life for a short time but had filled him with intrigue. 'Well, a farm shop and cafeteria are a must. Also, a community allotment would be a good way of getting the locals mixing with each other in the fresh air. Then, at Christmas, we could have a lights trail and horse-drawn carriage rides to visit Santa. They are just a few of my suggestions.'

Kerstin raised her eyebrows. 'Wow! Sounds like you are full of good ideas. Good luck with getting planning permission, or whatever you farmers need, for that.'

Mikey alleviated Kerstin's concerns. 'My father had taken Lawrie's ideas on board before he passed. We've had approval for what we need to do.'

Chloe was impressed. 'I'd love to see your farm. Is it far from London?'

Mikey's eyes lit up. 'Well, it only took me forty minutes to get here this afternoon, even with a quick stop at the bank. I'll pick you up at the weekend and take you down there if you like?'

Chloe giggled. 'That would be great!'

Lawrie had a better idea, 'Why don't I drive Sasha and Chloe to the farm on Saturday, and you can have one of your big brunches ready for us?' Lawrie winked at Chloe. 'Mikey's a great chef, you know.'

Kerstin felt left out. 'What about me?'

Adam placed an arm around her shoulders. 'You won't be available. I'm taking you for a river cruise on the Thames and then to the theatre.'

Kerstin placed her head on Adam's shoulder and glanced into his deep blue eyes. 'OK.'

Oswald was becoming bored of all the flirting going on around the table. 'Well, as you're all busy on Saturday, I suggest we meet at the Wensley International for lunch on Sunday. Sasha can tinkle the ivories before or after she's eaten. It's her choice.'

11

BACK TO WORK

Sasha felt exhausted. The last few days had left her head spinning. Now she had to get up, go to work *and* think of an excuse for why she took yesterday afternoon off sick. Sasha turned over and sank her face into the softness of her pillow. She would lie in for another five minutes before dragging herself out of bed and pulling on one of her new outfits, the thought of which brought trepidation rather than pleasure – Sasha's clothes had been bought with stolen cash.

The thought of the remaining ill-gotten gains under Chloe's bed increased her blood pressure. Then there was her ex-grandfather – Sasha felt sick when she thought of him. Sasha turned over onto her back and then sat up with a start; she could smell fried bacon. The girls never had time to cook in the mornings.

Kerstin wouldn't want to smell of bacon when she got to work. It must be Chloe.

Walking into the kitchen with her stomach rumbling, Sasha was met by a surprise: Adam in his black boxer shorts. Sasha tied the belt on her dressing gown into a knot and stopped herself from questioning whether he'd stayed overnight; the answer was obvious. Adam turned to smile at her. 'There's enough for everyone. I thought it was the least I could do after you girls put me up again for the night. Would you like ketchup or brown sauce on yours?'

Sasha sat down at the kitchen table. 'Ketchup, please.' She wasn't happy about Kerstin having Adam stay over on Sunday and Monday night without asking permission from her flatmates. Chloe was the next to arrive in the kitchen; she was fully dressed and sat beside Sasha. Adam played music through Kerstin's mini sound system and whistled while he cooked.

Sasha glared at Chloe before whispering, 'Did you know he was staying again last night?'

Chloe blushed before whispering back, 'I wasn't informed, but I heard he was here. Kerstin's room's next to mine, and the walls are thin.'

Sasha's eyes widened. 'Oh, please spare me the details! Did it go on for long?'

Chloe shook her head. 'They were talking for a bit

but kept their voices low. All I could make out was that Adam's staying with anybody and everybody until his new place is ready.'

Sasha tutted. 'Well, Kerstin should have asked our permission before moving someone in.'

Adam called over to Chloe, 'Morning! Ketchup or brown sauce?'

Chloe diverted her eyes from his smooth-shaven, bare chest. 'Ketchup, please.'

Kerstin sashayed into the kitchen in a tailored black suit and white blouse. She held out a pink dressing gown for Adam to squeeze his thick tattooed arms into. 'You'll need to bring your own next time. It's not good for the girls' blood pressure to wake up to a whistling naked chef.'

Adam laughed. 'I'm not naked.'

Kerstin reached up and kissed his cheek. 'I've no time for breakfast, I'm afraid. I have a shareholders' meeting at nine o'clock. I need to get in early. I'll grab something on the way.'

That left Sasha and Chloe sitting opposite a strapping rugby-playing hunk of a man in a pink dressing gown, which didn't go all the way around him. Adam munched on his double round of bacon sandwiches while turning his thoughts to Blake. 'I'll give Blake a call today to see how he's doing after the loss of his grandfather.'

Sasha and Chloe stuttered, 'Oh … oh … that's nice.'

Adam stared at Sasha, 'What an amazing coincidence you both originate from Durham and that your grandfathers ended up in the same care home.'

Sasha felt agitated. Why did there have to be a connection between Adam and Blake? There were too many people in the loop already who knew of Grandpa Wilf's link to the stash of cash. She stared back at Adam, 'Promise me you won't mention the cash – to Blake or to anybody.'

Adam held out his hand to shake Sasha's and felt a jolt of electricity. She felt it, too; he could see it in her sparkling blue eyes. He couldn't deny it – he'd always preferred blondes. He held Sasha's hand until Chloe interrupted the "moment". 'Thanks for breakfast, Adam. Sasha and I should get ready for work now. We'll need to lock you out before we go, so we'll tidy the kitchen while you return Kerstin's dressing gown and put some clothes on.'

*

Sasha's mind wasn't on her job. It was on the best bacon sandwich she'd ever tasted. Lawrie glanced over at her smiling face as she dealt with one disgruntled caller after another. She was a different woman from the one he'd spent most of yesterday with. He wondered if she'd patched things up with her grandfather or if she was excited about playing the piano again on Sunday at the Wensley International. He doubted it was his suggestion to take her to the farm. She hadn't looked at him all morning. Something had brought a glow to Sasha's cheeks, and he couldn't work out what.

At four o'clock, Sasha's phone flashed up with a message:

> *I've spoken to Blake, and I need to update you. I'll meet you outside the call centre after work. What time's best? Adam*

Sasha messaged back:

> *Just after 5.00, if that suits you.*

Adam responded:

> *Perfect.*

Sasha's stomach somersaulted. She grabbed her bag and went to the Ladies' cloakroom to brush her hair and freshen her makeup. That way, she could dash out of work in less than an hour.

Lawrie perched himself on the edge of Sasha's desk just before five o'clock. 'Fancy a drink after work? I've seen Adam lurking around outside. He'll be waiting for me to finish so we can go for a pint.'

Sasha's heart sank. She wouldn't escape from the office and fall into Adam's massive arms with Lawrie in tow. Sasha rubbed her forehead; not only was she being silly, but she was also being a bad friend to Kerstin – if only in her thoughts. Lawrie had just saved her from making a fool of herself. Sasha took a deep breath before responding, 'A drink with you and Adam would be great.'

If Adam was surprised that Sasha walked out of the building with Lawrie, he didn't show it. Lawrie slapped his friend on the back. 'Great idea of yours to take me out for a pint; we have a little hanger-on. You don't mind if Sasha joins us, do you?'

Adam shook his head as he held Sasha's gaze. 'They say two's company, but three's a crowd. We may as well be a crowd.'

Lawrie reached for his phone. 'Another great idea! I'll invite Oswald and Rafferty; they're in London today. Sasha can invite Chloe and Kerstin too.'

Adam's body stiffened. 'Don't do that. I have some information I need to share with Sasha, and I'd rather do that in private.'

Lawrie raised his eyebrows. 'That sounds interesting. It's a good job I invited Sasha along then. Let's get to the pub, and you can tell us your news.'

12

INTRIGUING INFORMATION

Adam was wearing smart jeans and a white shirt. He looked even more handsome than when he'd left the apartment this morning in a navy suit. Sasha was impressed with how well he was keeping up appearances despite the fact he was bed-hopping. Sasha removed that thought from her mind; Adam was house-swapping, temporarily apartment-sharing, doing the best he could while he was in the process of moving.

Lawrie went to the bar to buy the drinks, and Adam leaned forward to whisper to Sasha, giving her a whiff of expensive aftershave, 'I can't tell you the news while Lawrie's around.' Sasha breathed in the heady aroma of musk; Kerstin was so lucky.

Lawrie placed Sasha's wineglass on the table and went back to pick up the pints. Sasha stared at Adam. 'What are we going to do?'

Adam winked, highlighting his deep blue eyes and long black lashes. 'Leave it with me.'

Lawrie sat down. 'Go on, you can tell us the news now. We're sworn to secrecy.'

Adam sipped his pint before speaking, 'Kerstin's in trouble.'

Sasha gasped. 'What kind of trouble?'

Adam sat back in his chair. 'I was talking to Blake this afternoon; he's found his rugby kit in the bottom of his grandfather's wardrobe.'

Sasha gasped again. 'Is Blake back in Durham?'

'Yes, he went home to be with his family during such a sad time. He's only staying tonight, then he'll go back again for the funeral at the end of the month.'

Sasha cringed. Kerstin really was in trouble; she'd lied to Blake about putting his kit in a charity collection bag. How could they get her out of this one?

Lawrie shrugged. 'I don't see a problem. Blake will just think Kerstin's weird and avoid her like the plague if you ever take her to the rugby club. There's little chance they'll bump into each other again. Blake will just be pleased he's got his kit back.'

Sasha could see Lawrie's point; she was also pleased Adam had managed to steer him away from whatever news was meant for her ears only. She turned to Lawrie. 'Adam was right to want to tell me in private. We should keep this between ourselves. What Kerstin doesn't know won't hurt her. Now, Adam, will you be staying at ours again tonight?'

Lawrie's head swivelled to stare at his friend. 'You're laying it on a bit thick, aren't you, mate? Staying over at your new girlfriend's place in the first week. It's not like you to be so keen.'

Adam lowered his eyes. 'It's not what it seems. Kerstin's been kind enough to give me a floor to sleep on. Oswald and Rafferty were getting fed up with me lodging with them until I get the keys to my new apartment. There's only a couple of weeks until I move my things out of storage and become self-sufficient again.'

Lawrie was surprised he hadn't realised his friend's predicament. 'You should have said. There are spare rooms at ours. Mum won't mind putting you up. Let's finish our drinks, then we'll go and give her the good news. We can't have you living out of a storage unit and sleeping on floors.'

Sasha didn't like the sound of that; she had a better

idea, 'If it's only for a couple of weeks, then Adam should stay with us. He can sleep on the sofa instead of in Kerstin's room. Besides, Adam's toothbrush and overnight bag are still at ours.'

Adam blushed. He didn't like being talked about as if he wasn't in the room. He also didn't like the mess he was in. Adam had been giving Kerstin all the wrong signals. He should have made a beeline for Sasha on Sunday night. When he thought back to it, the most fun he'd had was when he'd spent time alone with her at the casino. Adam needed to get his self-respect back – and quick! He reached for his phone and booked a room online at the Wensley International before finishing his pint.

Lawrie finished his pint, too. 'Come along, let's go to mine.'

Sasha stood up. 'It's your choice, Adam. Lawrie's place or mine?'

Adam smiled. 'We'll pop to Sasha's first to collect my overnight things; then I'll be off to the Wensley International. I've booked a room for a couple of weeks. I don't know why I didn't consider staying in a hotel before.'

*

Sasha's knees trembled as she walked into the Wensley International. She didn't know if it was the sight of the grand piano on the mezzanine floor above reception or that Adam had messaged her and asked her to come to Room 643 for dinner at eight o'clock. *Something* was making her heart pound, and her legs turn to jelly. Sasha headed for the lift and pressed the button for the sixth floor. She was soon standing outside Adam's room, giving a light knock on the door.

Adam smiled at the sight of Sasha, who had now changed out of her work clothes and was wearing a red off-the-shoulder cocktail dress with a diamante belt. She did a twirl before chatting away, 'Is this a bit much for dinner in your room? I bought it on Sunday and don't know when I'll get another chance to wear it. I went a bit mad when I thought I was rich.'

Adam pulled Sasha into his arms and stopped her nervous chatter by planting a kiss on her lips. Sasha kept her eyes open – was she dreaming? Adam pulled away with a large smile on his face. Sasha stared at his perfect white teeth. This sort of thing only happened in movies. What would Kerstin say? What would Chloe say? Sasha really couldn't care what her friends would say as she reached up and kissed Adam again.

Adam led Sasha to the sofa while running his hands through her long blonde hair. Several kisses later, there was a knock on the door. 'Room Service!' A member of staff wheeled a trolley into the room. 'Would you like your meal inside or outside on the balcony, Sir?'

Sasha's eyes widened as she took in the sight of the room around her. It had a balcony? Admittedly, she'd only been there for ten minutes, but she hadn't seen past the designer stubble on Adam's handsome face. Adam glanced out of the floor-to-ceiling window. 'It's a warm evening. We'll eat outside.'

Adam's foot touched Sasha's under the table, and she thought back to Sunday lunchtime and her envy of the lovers in the bistro. What a turnaround for the books! Just this morning, Adam was Kerstin's – now he was hers. Sasha didn't want to think about the fallout when her friends found out; she just wanted to live in the moment.

After two glasses of champagne, Sasha remembered why Adam had wanted to get her on her own. 'What's the secret information that only *I* should hear about?'

Adam reached across the table and clasped Sasha's hand. 'Blake said your grandfather's into drugs.'

Sasha burst out laughing. 'Grandpa Wilf won't even take a paracetamol. He's drugs-free.'

Adam locked eyes with Sasha. 'Rupert told Blake your grandfather's a drug dealer.'

This time, Sasha was doubled over with the giggles. 'What made Rupert think that?'

'Because Blake found a packet of white substance

in his grandfather's tea caddy at the care home, and Rupert said it belonged to Wilf.'

Sasha turned white. Any worry she'd had about Blake being angry with Kerstin or Kerstin being livid with her paled into insignificance. 'I must get to the bottom of this. I'll go to Durham at the weekend.'

Adam squeezed her hand. 'I'll come with you.'

'Why?'

'Because I want to make myself scarce while Kerstin ditches me for Blake.'

'What?'

'They'd be perfect together. I just need to make them see it. I'll give the river cruise and theatre tickets to Blake, and he can turn up instead of me. I'll leave it up to him to decide if he wants to challenge Kerstin about his rugby kit.'

Sasha smiled. 'OK, but we'll need to go there and back on Saturday. We're all having lunch here on Sunday, remember?'

Adam kissed Sasha's hand. 'How could I forget? That just leaves Lawrie.'

'Lawrie?'

'He has the hots for you, and you're supposed to be

going to the farm on Saturday.'

Sasha cringed. 'I forgot about the farm. How embarrassing; Lawrie's not my type.'

Adam grinned. 'Lawrie will be fine once he's back on the farm. You've just been an exciting distraction. How many angels fall from heaven and start playing the piano to a rapturous audience in the middle of St Pancras? Most of the men in the station were mesmerised by you on Sunday.'

'You weren't mesmerised.'

'I was. I just didn't dare hope I'd be good enough for you. Especially when you outshone all the ladies in the casino, too.'

Sasha pushed her chair back and went to sit on Adam's lap. 'Blake had better do a good job on Saturday, then we can come clean about us.'

Adam stroked Sasha's cheek. 'There's no rush.'

13

MONEY BAGS

Sasha stood before her grandfather, who was shocked at her surprise visit. 'Tell me where the money came from.'

Grandpa Wilf raised his hands in the air. 'I've told you before, Sasha. It's your inheritance.'

Sasha stamped her foot. 'Just tell me the truth! I can't believe all that money was yours. Are you a drug dealer?'

'Why are you asking that?'

'Because Blake found a packet of white substance in his grandfather's tea caddy, and Rupert said it belonged to you.'

'Well, I never. Crafty old Rupert. I can't speak ill

of the dead. So, I will keep my mouth shut.'

Grandpa Wilf walked into his kitchen and, with a shaking hand, poured a large glass of brandy – for medicinal purposes, of course. It wasn't good for him to be under so much stress. If Sasha found out how he'd obtained the money, she'd disown him. If her mother found out, *she'd* kill him. Grandpa Wilf was a dead man walking. Bearing that in mind and knowing he didn't have long left, with the brandy giving him courage, he made up a story.

'Now, Sasha, what I'm going to tell you will come as a shock. I've never been a fan of your mother's – I much preferred your father. He was a decent man and still is.'

Sasha gulped. 'Still is? Have you heard from him?'

'We've never lost touch. Your mother turned him into a monster in your eyes. He had a brief dalliance while they were still married, but I didn't blame him. Angela's had another man on the go for years. Where do you think she goes to every Saturday? Her hair never looks any different.'

Sasha stuttered, 'Mum … Mum … never came to my ballet shows or piano concerts if they were on Saturday afternoons.'

'Exactly. Not even when you played at the Royal Albert Hall.'

'You and Dad came to that.'

Grandpa Wilf dropped his head. 'Anyway, your father and I came up with a plan to cut your mother out of the loop and benefit you.'

'What plan?'

'I withdrew my savings and gave them to your father. I didn't want Angela getting her hands on my money. Your father's been shrewd with my investments, and he recently cashed them in. So, there! That's how I became rich.'

Sasha sighed. 'You didn't need to go through all this secrecy – you could have made a Will.'

Grandpa Wilf was tired of spinning a yarn that Sasha wasn't accepting. He just hoped she'd stop interrogating him and spend the money before it was too late.

Sasha stood up and paced around Grandpa Wilf's living room. 'How am I going to look my mother in the eyes anymore? How can I forgive her? She made me hate my father so much that I lost contact with him. I took her side in all this, and she's been lying to me all my life!'

Grandpa Wilf patted the seat next to him. 'Sit down, Sasha. Angela married the wrong man. She's had a lifetime of unhappiness because of it. She's been living a lie that she wants none of us to know about, and we need to keep it that way.'

Sasha's eyes widened. 'Why? How?'

'Because Angela's my daughter. I don't want any fallouts with my flesh and blood. Your grandmother would never forgive me. God rest her soul.'

The sports bag sprang to Sasha's mind. 'How did you get hold of the sports bag?'

'Well, I didn't think Rupert was coming back after he went to hospital, so I rummaged around in his apartment to see if he had a bag you could take the money away in.'

Sasha was calming down. A weight had lifted; her father hadn't deserted her when she was fifteen. Her mother was suffering for her sins, and Sasha felt pleased about that. Her grandfather wasn't a drug dealer; she allowed herself a little smile at the absurdity of the thought. And the money under Chloe's bed was really Sasha's. It was her inheritance from her grandfather that her father had invested wisely. She was too tired to question the legality of their financial dealings but trusted her father to keep things above board.

'When can I see my father? I need to thank him.'

Grandpa Wilf shook his head. 'It's best to leave

things be, Sasha. Too much time has passed. Just go back to London and spend, spend, spend. If you bump into your father, promise me you'll not mention this conversation.'

Sasha's eyes widened. 'My father lives in London?'

Grandpa Wilf chose to keep quiet. He'd dug a big enough hole for himself already. His heart went out to Sasha. The part of the story about her mother was true. The part he'd told her about her father was not. Ted wasn't a good sort. Grandpa Wilf had only thrown him into the conversation to get Sasha to accept the money.

A smile lit up Sasha's face. 'Please ask my father, if he's available, to meet me at the Wensley International Hotel at four o'clock tomorrow afternoon.'

Grandpa Wilf reached for a pen and wrote on the back of an old envelope. There was no way he could risk Sasha meeting her father again. Besides, Ted had shown no interest in her for the last seven years. He wouldn't turn up even if the message were passed on. Grandpa Wilf tried to sound sincere as he folded the envelope and put it in his pocket, 'Where will you be in the hotel?'

Sasha felt a rush of excitement run through her veins. 'My father will find me.'

*

Adam stood up when he saw Sasha running towards him. 'Have you had a successful afternoon?'

Sasha beamed. 'More successful than you could ever imagine. I'm sorry it took so long. You've been waiting at the station for hours.'

Adam shrugged his shoulders. 'It didn't seem that long. I went for a walk and then popped into the bookstore to buy a book, which I've been reading in the coffee shop for the past couple of hours. It's been a nice relaxing afternoon.'

The train was waiting at the platform, so the couple climbed on. Adam held Sasha's hand. 'So, is your grandfather a drug dealer?'

Sasha giggled. 'Far from it. He's an unwavering patriarch of our family. I should never have doubted him. He taught me everything happens for a reason and that keeping secrets is sometimes the best thing to do.'

Adam sat down next to Sasha before raising his eyebrows. 'I'm not sure about that. I've always believed that honesty is the best policy.'

Adam's phone vibrated with a message from Blake:

> *Your plan worked! Kerstin much prefers me to you – and I'm not complaining!*

Adam showed the message to Sasha, and she did a little clap. 'Ask Blake if he mentioned his rugby kit.'

Blake responded:

> *Kerstin said it must have been Adam's kit as he'd been staying over recently. She'd got confused as there were so many clothes she gave to charity. I know she's lying, but there must be a reason for it. I've forgiven her already.*

Sasha raised her eyebrows. 'See, the odd white lie does no harm.'

It was Sasha's turn to receive a message – from Kerstin:

> *Adam didn't tell me where he is today, but I guess he's with you – Blake says Adam prefers blondes. Tell Adam the substitute he sent today is in the team for the rest of the season and that **he** has been well and truly dropped.*

The next message to ping through to Sasha was from Chloe:

> *We've had a brilliant day. I want to live on the farm! How is Grandpa Wilf? Please tell me he's not a drug baron. Chloe xx*

Sasha messaged Chloe and Kerstin:

Grandpa Wilf's in the clear. The money's legit. I'll see you both in the morning. I'll not be home tonight. Love Sasha xxx

Sasha showed the message to Adam. 'Wow! Your grandfather's in the clear, and the money's legit!'

Sasha winked. 'You missed the bit about "I'll not be home tonight".'

Adam slid an arm around Sasha's shoulders before kissing her. 'I already knew that.'

14

LUNCH AT THE WENSLEY

Sasha opened her apartment door to the sight of Chloe and Kerstin trying on outfits. Kerstin held up a pale pink jumpsuit and turned to face Sasha. 'Do you think this will be OK to wear to the Wensley?'

Sasha walked over to hug her friend. 'I'm sorry about Adam. I hope you're OK about it. Blake seems very nice.'

Kerstin hugged Sasha back. 'Things never got off the ground between Adam and me. I should have known he preferred you when he left me on my own at the casino. Besides, Blake is gorgeous! I've invited him to join us for lunch today.'

Chloe held up the off-the-shoulder red dress Sasha had worn the other night. 'You don't mind if I borrow this, do you? I expect you'll be in your gold evening dress, ready for your performance on the piano.'

Sasha was relieved her friends weren't holding a grudge against her. She couldn't bear to be without them. She responded to Chloe, 'I can't wear the evening dress for lunch. I'll get changed into it after we've eaten. You can borrow my red dress if you loan me your lilac midi dress. We should go shopping again soon to top up our wardrobes. It's such a relief to have the pressure off in respect of my finances.'

Chloe giggled. 'It's a deal.'

*

Lunch at the Wensley International was a treat for everyone. As regulars there, Oswald and Rafferty took the grandeur of the occasion in their stride. Lawrie was taken aback to see Kerstin with Blake and Sasha with Adam. He tried to eat, but every mouthful was difficult to swallow. Lawrie was annoyed with himself for falling so hard for a girl who would never look twice at him; the sooner he moved to the farm, the better.

Sasha must have read his thoughts. 'What's keeping you from making the move to the farm? You don't need to work in the call centre for free to keep your mother happy.'

Lawrie lowered his eyes. 'You're right. My mother won't even notice I've gone. No one will.'

Blake leaned across the table to speak to Sasha, 'Have you got the cuckoo clock working yet?'

Sasha shook her head. 'I wouldn't know where to start.'

Blake gave a dimpled smile. 'I could have a look at it if you like. I've fixed a few watches in my time. A clock shouldn't be too different. Although I've never had to bring a cuckoo back to life before.'

There were chuckles around the table, and Sasha was grateful for the suggestion. 'That would be great, thanks, Blake.'

Adam nudged Sasha before whispering, 'Are you OK? You've hardly eaten anything.' Sasha's stomach was churning. There wasn't long to wait now until she was reunited with her father after seven years.

After coffee and liqueurs, Oswald requested the bill. The waiter held his hand up. 'Full payment has been received for your meal. We hope you found it satisfactory.'

All eyes turned to Sasha, who blushed. 'It wasn't me.' Her heart was pounding. Her father must be here already. Who else would have paid for the meal?

Oswald rubbed his hands together. 'Who are *we* to complain? One of us must have an admirer – a rich one at that. Now Sasha, darling, you need to get changed before your performance.'

Sasha checked the time on Adam's watch while scanning the room for her father. 'It's only just after three; I'll be performing at four. My dress is upstairs in Adam's room, so I'll pop up there in a few minutes.'

Oswald and Rafferty exchanged glances before staring at Adam. Oswald spoke first, 'We thought you were staying with Kerstin.'

Rafferty glanced at Blake. 'I'm sure you know Adam was sleeping on Kerstin's bedroom floor.' He then turned to Adam, 'If the floor wasn't comfortable, you should have come back to stay with us. It must be costing you a fortune staying here.'

Adam blushed. 'I was fed up imposing myself on everyone. It's been fine here; my apartment will be ready soon.'

Sasha couldn't see her father anywhere. She pushed her chair back and stood up. 'Please excuse me. I'll go and get changed.'

Oswald did a little clap. 'Will the angel from heaven be landing on the mezzanine floor, or will she be gracing us with her presence in the bar first?'

Sasha's head was spinning, she felt sick, she couldn't do this, could she? What if she saw her father and froze during a classical piece? Anything, absolutely anything, could go wrong at four o'clock. She was in a daze as she headed for the lift, clutching Adam's room key.

Oswald raised his eyebrows. 'Sasha's getting into character. She'll go straight to the piano when she's all glammed up. We need to get onto the mezzanine floor in good time so I can adjust her dress before I start filming. Let's go to the bar for a quick one to calm our nerves.'

Rafferty glanced at Oswald. 'What are you like? Sasha's the only one with nerves.'

Oswald held onto his chest. 'My heart's pounding for her. This is going to be Sasha's big break. I've asked Paulo to wedge the entrance doors open. Sasha's talent will be heard as far as Hyde Park. Paulo's arranged for extra bar staff to cope with the influx of tourists.'

Adam shifted in his seat. Not only did he believe in honesty, but he also believed in fate. Adam had a very good idea who'd paid the meal bill, but he didn't dare hope he was right. He stood up. 'I'll meet you all in the bar. I need a stiff one.'

15

THE ANGEL FROM HEAVEN

P aulo stood at the entrance to the hotel. He wanted to assess how far the music could be heard once the pianist began her recital. He'd seen Oswald's video of Sasha's performance at St Pancras, and he was quite excited the grand piano on the mezzanine floor was about to be brought to life. Paulo stepped outside into the sunshine and crossed over the road. The hotel was impressive with its numerous flagpoles and bountiful floral displays. Two concierge team members wearing top hats flanked the open doorway, and Paulo hoped with all his heart that this afternoon would be the beginning of happier times for Mr Wensley.

There it was – the music had begun. Paulo breathed in deeply; he recognised the piece as *Chopin's Spring Waltz*. It was exquisite. As anticipated, tourists gathered outside the hotel to savour the free performance. A hand rested on Paulo's shoulder. 'Thank you for inviting me.'

Paulo turned, then bowed. 'Mr Wensley. I hoped you would come.'

The tall, tanned, white-haired gentleman removed his silk handkerchief from his pocket and dabbed at his deep blue eyes. 'I never thought I would see this day. The hotel has come to life.'

Paulo held his shoulders back. 'I anticipated an influx of tourists, so I arranged for extra bar staff.'

Mr Wensley patted Paulo on the back. 'Good thinking. We should invite everyone inside. Instruct the kitchen to rustle up some canapés and bowls of nuts. I'll head over the road to mingle with our guests.'

Paulo took the unprecedented move of grabbing Mr Wensley's arm before staring into his eyes. 'Are you sure about this? Are you ready to face the public again? It's only been five years since Mrs Wensley passed.'

Mr Wensley patted Paulo's hand. 'Five years without listening to piano music has been far too long. My darling wife would be thrilled to know her beloved grand piano is in the safe hands of such a gifted musician.'

Adam ran down the stairs from the mezzanine floor to greet Mr Wensley. He took him into a bear hug. 'Grandfather! You're back from Dubai. I can't believe you're here. You paid our lunch bill, didn't you?'

Mr Wensley nodded. 'I certainly did. I'll also be settling the bill for your room. It's good to see you, Adam. I'm afraid I've stayed away for far too long. I'm back now and looking forward to making up for lost time.' Mr Wensley stared up at the mezzanine floor. 'Do you know the young lady who's playing the piano?'

Adam smiled. 'I certainly do. Sasha's my girlfriend. I can't wait for you to meet her. It could be a while, though. She's only just started playing, and once she starts, she can't stop.'

Thirty minutes later, Sasha was interrupted by a young girl sliding onto the stool to sit next to her. Sasha's trance was broken. 'Do you know any Disney songs?' The girl's mother stepped forward, grabbed her daughter's arm, lifted her off the stool, and apologised profusely.

Sasha smiled at the little girl. 'Do you play the piano?'

The girl nodded vigorously. 'Yes. I'm six, and I started last week. I'm not as good as you, though.'

Nervous laughter rippled through the shocked audience. Sasha moved to the edge of the stool and patted the space next to her so the girl could sit down again. 'Now watch closely while I play. This is a tune I learnt when I wasn't much older than you.'

Sasha then played a simple version of *When You Wish Upon a Star*. When she finished, the crowd burst into rapturous applause. The girl's mother whisked her daughter away while smiling her gratitude at Sasha. A voice called from the enthusiastic crowd, 'Any chance of *Younger Than Springtime* from *South Pacific*?'

Sasha was happy to oblige, and Oswald was thrilled. He handed his phone to Lawrie to continue recording Sasha's performance before grabbing Rafferty. 'Let's get the dancing started.' With couples twirling around the mezzanine floor, in the foyer and out on the pavement, Mr Wensley knew he had a hit on his hands. He turned to Adam. 'I'll offer Sasha a job for as long as she wants. She's good with children, can turn her hand to any type of music and is very easy on the eye to boot.'

Adam laughed. 'Great idea, Sasha will make an excellent resident pianist.'

Sasha played three more popular tunes, then stood up and curtseyed to signify the end of her performance. She wasn't in a zone like she had been at St Pancras. She was concerned about finding her father. Mr Wensley walked up to Sasha and held his hand to his heart. 'That was the most exquisite performance I have ever heard. My wife was a pianist, and since she died, this hotel had lost its heart. Today, you brought it back to life, and I will be forever grateful. Starting with offering you a position here for as long as you wish.'

A blonde middle-aged man with streaks of silver in his hair approached Sasha from behind. 'You will need to speak to her manager first.'

Sasha turned around and flung herself into her father's arms. 'Dad! You're here. I've missed you so much.'

Sasha's father kissed the top of his daughter's head while shoving his wallet into his pocket. Paying a waiter twenty pounds for *this* tip-off had been worth every penny. He'd seen the video of Sasha online and had been trying to track her down. Ted gave a sickly grin to Mr Wensley. 'I'm sure you will agree; there's a wealth of interest in my daughter's talent since the video of her playing at St Pancras station went viral. I need to ensure Sasha accepts the best deals for her. Not necessarily monetary ones, but ones that will bring her the happiness she deserves.'

Sasha whispered in her father's ear, 'Thank you for the money.'

Ted frowned. What money? He decided to keep quiet; he didn't want anything to ruin the opportunity he had before him to make some easy cash. All the time he'd invested in taking Sasha to piano lessons was finally going to pay off!

Chloe and Kerstin were standing with mouths open and eyebrows raised. Why was Sasha hugging a middle-aged man? Adam walked over to enlighten them. 'The man's her father.'

Kerstin turned to Chloe. 'Well, I never. What's Sasha going to surprise us with next?'

Blake and Mikey arrived with glasses of wine for the girls. Blake kissed Kerstin's cheek. 'You needn't tell me now, but when you're ready, why did you lie to me about my rugby kit?'

Kerstin looked into Blake's eyes. 'I was protecting my friend. My apologies – I won't lie again.'

Blake's piercing blue eyes lit up as he slid an arm around Kerstin's waist. 'I'm delighted to hear that.'

16

OPPORTUNITIES

Adam offered Sasha and her father the privacy of his room for a catch-up. They sat on the balcony overlooking Hyde Park and reflected on their seven years apart.

Sasha had questions, 'Why didn't you let me know where you'd gone? Have you been living in London all this time? Why did you go without saying goodbye to me?'

Ted reached out to hold his daughter's hand. 'I wrote to you many times, but your mother must have intercepted my letters. When you didn't respond, I thought you'd disowned me.'

Sasha sighed, 'What a mess. I didn't find out until yesterday that my mother's been having an affair for years. Grandpa Wilf told me. When did *you* find out about it?'

'When you were very young. I tolerated it for as long as possible to keep our family together.'

Sasha narrowed her eyes. 'I'll never speak to my mother again.'

Ted squeezed his daughter's hand. 'You're angry now, but you'll forgive Angela eventually.' Sasha wasn't sure about that. Ted continued, 'Anyway, in answer to your question, I've been living in London since I left Durham.'

Sasha gasped, 'I went to university in London; that's where I met my flatmates.'

Ted smiled. 'I know. Wilf kept me informed of your progress. You looked amazing on your Graduation Day.'

'You were there?!'

Ted lowered his eyes as he continued to lie, 'I wouldn't have missed it for the world. I watched from a distance so you didn't see me – I didn't want to spoil your special day. I'm so proud of you, Sasha.'

Sasha had questions for her father, 'What about *you*? Are you still working for the newspaper?'

Ted held his shoulders back. 'Yes, I'm a senior reporter now.'

'Are you married?'

Ted shook his head. 'Never again. Once bitten, twice shy. Now, that's enough about me. What are we going to do with *you*? Are you interested in working at this hotel?'

Sasha gasped. She'd completely forgotten about the tall, tanned, white-haired gentleman. 'How do I know that was a proper job offer? It could have been someone having a laugh.'

Ted grinned. 'It's wise to be suspicious, but I can vouch for Mr Wensley. The newspaper has run several articles on him in the past. He's been reclusive since his wife died. News of your performance brought him back from Dubai. I don't see any harm in accepting his offer in the interim period before you're inundated with record deals, demands for concert tours, magazine shoots, etc. I'll negotiate your package for the Wensley. I won't have my daughter doing things on the cheap. You can trust *me* to get the best deals for the both of us.'

Sasha giggled. 'You're joking.'

Ted kept a straight face. 'I'm serious, Sasha. You have a gift that can take you wherever you want to go. And I'll be here with you all the way. I want to protect my daughter and make up for lost time.'

Sasha felt a warm feeling encompass her. It was such a relief to have her father back. 'Let's go downstairs. I want to introduce you to my friends.'

Ted stood up and held out his arm for his daughter to slide her hand through. 'It was very good of your boyfriend to lend us his room for our catch-up.'

Sasha caught her breath. 'How do you know Adam's my boyfriend?'

'Well, he told his grandfather you're his girlfriend, so I guess that makes him your boyfriend.'

Sasha's eyes widened. 'Adam's grandfather's here?'

Ted raised an eyebrow. 'How long have you been with Adam?'

Sasha blushed. 'Only since Tuesday.'

Ted's eyes twinkled. 'Ah, I see. A new romance. At least Adam didn't try to win you over by divulging his family connection.'

Sasha frowned. 'His family connection?'

Ted held his daughter's gaze as he enlightened her, 'Adam is Mr Wensley's grandson. That shouldn't make a difference to you accepting Mr Wensley's job offer, but it might prove difficult if you split up.'

Sasha was in shock. There was so much to take in. She let her father guide her out of Adam's room and into the lift. When the doors opened onto the mezzanine floor, she was met by cheers and whistles. The entrance doors to the hotel had been closed, and as Sasha glanced down to the foyer, she could see cameras flashing outside. The warm feeling she had just experienced gave way to shivers throughout her body.

She whispered to her father before her knees gave way, 'I don't want this. Why can't they leave me alone?'

Adam rushed over to her. 'Are you OK? You've gone white.'

Rafferty placed a chair behind Sasha, and Ted lowered her onto it. 'We need to give my daughter some space. It's been a very taxing day for her. One of her so-called friends must have tipped off the vultures outside.'

Mr Wensley ensured the mezzanine floor was cleared, and as soon as Sasha felt well enough to stand, he asked Ted to take her back up to Adam's room. 'We need to give the paparazzi time to disperse, then I'll arrange for a car to pick you both up from the back entrance so you can take Sasha home.'

Mr Wensley walked outside to speak to the eager photographers. 'You may as well go home. The young lady won't be leaving the hotel today.'

One news reporter challenged that statement,

'That's not what we've been told. Her father said she'd be up for speaking to the press. He tipped us off. Ted's keen to promote her. Tabloids tomorrow, prime time TV later in the week.'

Lawrie glared at Adam. 'We need to stop this. Sasha would hate the publicity.'

Adam nodded. 'I agree; I'll speak to my grandfather. He'll know what to do.'

Thirty minutes later, Mr Wensley knocked on Adam's room to be greeted by Ted. 'I wondered if you would join me for dinner. I feel a bit peckish, and your daughter needs to rest. Come with me, and you can tell me all about your rise to fame at the newspaper. I remember you from when you were a novice reporter. You interviewed me back in the day.'

Ted ran a hand through his hair. 'That's very kind of you. I've climbed the ranks since the last time we met. Maybe you can give me an exclusive about your return to the hotel today after so long away. Had you been tipped off that my daughter would be performing?'

Mr Wensley didn't like Ted at all. 'I don't live my life by reacting to "tip-offs". With all due respect to your daughter, she isn't the reason I'm back in London.' That wasn't true; if it hadn't been for Paulo making Mr Wensley aware of Sasha's recital, he'd still be in Dubai. Still, it was the jolt Mr Wensley needed to return to normality, so he was more than happy to provide Ted with some obscure story while Adam protected his girlfriend from her underhand father.

17

LIES UNCOVERED

With her father out of the way, Adam and Lawrie were in the uncomfortable position of advising Sasha of their concerns for her welfare.

Adam sat on the sofa next to her, clasping her hands. 'How do you feel about all of this?'

Sasha's head was thumping. 'There's so much to take in. Why didn't you tell me your grandfather owned this hotel?'

Adam blushed, 'I hadn't told anyone. It's a shock to all my friends. I wanted to build relationships with people on my own merit. Not because I've got a wealthy grandfather.'

Sasha could see Adam's point. He looked

crestfallen now the secret was out. 'Well, it was very kind of Mr Wensley to offer me a job, but he'll need to speak to my father about it. Dad has my best interests at heart. It's such a relief he turned up today. I'd be lost without him.'

Lawrie's blood pressure was rising, and he paced around the room. 'What *are* your best interests, Sasha? Do you want to be splattered all over the tabloids? Do you want to live in hiding, other than when you're on stage or on a television show? I overheard your father's plans for you, and I don't believe they're what you want. Your father is sacrificing your privacy for his own means. He'll be after a cut of your earnings as your manager.'

Sasha glared at Lawrie. 'You're so wrong. Dad was only making suggestions. It will be up to me to choose what I want to do. It was just unfortunate the paparazzi turned up earlier – Oswald will be to blame for that. All I want is to play the piano – I don't want to be famous.'

Lawrie let out a sigh of relief before crouching down in front of the sofa and staring into Sasha's eyes. 'It was your father who tipped off the paparazzi.'

Sasha gulped, and Adam squeezed her hands tighter, willing his strength to flow through to her. This was terrible news for Sasha, who had reconnected with her father only to find out she was and had been, better off without him.

Tears streamed down Sasha's face, and Adam handed her a handkerchief. Sasha blew her nose. 'What am I going to do?'

Lawrie began pacing again. 'We'll get you out of here without your father knowing where you've gone. You need time and space to decide what you want to do with your life without interference from people who are more interested in themselves.'

Adam stared at Lawrie. 'But what about the paparazzi? They'll track Sasha down.'

Lawrie stopped pacing. 'Not if Mikey takes Sasha to the farm.'

*

Sasha left the hotel via the back entrance in a delivery van, which also contained Adam and Mikey. The van dropped the trio off two streets away from Sasha's apartment block, where Mikey's car was parked. Adam grabbed Sasha's hand. 'Once we get to your apartment, you need to pack a few things to get you through the week. Mikey will drive you to the farm tonight, and I'll come to see you at the weekend.'

Sasha was in a daze. Was there no one in this world she could trust? Her mother was a liar, and so was her father. Grandpa Wilf was prone to lying, too.

He'd been in touch with her father all this time. Sasha decided then and there that she'd get rid of the remaining seven thousand pounds as soon as possible. She wanted nothing to do with the money connected to her dysfunctional family. Sasha had four thousand in her bank account from her casino winnings; that would suffice until she found another job.

*

The following morning, Sasha was awakened by Mikey knocking on her bedroom door. 'Breakfast is ready!'

Sasha checked the time; it was eleven o'clock. She couldn't believe she'd slept in for so long. She rubbed her eyes and reached for her dressing gown before heading downstairs to the farmhouse kitchen. Mikey placed a tray of fruit, yoghurt, pancakes and a full English Breakfast in front of her. Sasha's eyes widened. 'Is this for the both of us?'

Mikey laughed. 'No. I had my breakfast hours ago. I need to dash back to work. A delivery of fertiliser is arriving this morning. I want to make sure they offload it in the right place. We're clearing parts of the farm before the building work starts on Wednesday.'

Sasha sliced a sausage. 'Do you have many employees on the farm helping you?'

'There's always a selection of farm hands available. Work varies throughout the seasons. I'm lucky my dad built up a good team of reliable staff who've worked here for years. They're part of our family now.'

Sasha was pleased about that. She hated thinking that Mikey was alone, trying to cope with such a huge responsibility. 'That's good then. Is there anything I can do to help you today?'

Mikey turned to head outside. 'Just rest up and stay out of trouble until Lawrie arrives.'

Sasha placed her knife and fork down. 'Lawrie's coming here today?'

Mikey glanced over his shoulder. 'He certainly is. He's finally making the move. He'll be here by five o'clock.'

*

Sasha pulled on her denim shorts and a white t-shirt before venturing outside into the sunshine. She felt surprisingly content after the events of the weekend. They were now behind her, and she could look forward to her future, which she was determined would be brighter than her past.

Sasha shielded her eyes with her hand. She'd forgotten to pack her sunglasses in the rush last night. She could also do with a pair of wellies. It was summer, but she noticed most of the farm hands wearing wellies. She supposed parts of the farm in the shade down by the river would still be squelchy at this time of year. Sasha wanted to explore while she was here. Being outside made her feel relaxed. She walked over to Mikey. 'Are there any shops near here that sell sunglasses and wellies?'

Mikey pointed down the lane. 'There's a bus that stops down there every half hour. The first place you'll come to is the village centre. You won't find decent sunglasses there. If you stay on until the next stop, you'll end up in the nearest town. You'll be spoilt for choice in Market Furnley; there are designer shops galore.'

Sasha liked the sound of that. 'Do you need anything while I'm in town? Can I bring something back for dinner?'

Mikey shook his head. 'Dinner's all sorted. Lawrie's picking up a takeaway on his way here. I'll be starving by five o'clock. He says you're OK with Chinese.'

Sasha frowned. How did Lawrie know that? She waved to Mikey. 'I'll be back by half-four to set the table. See you later!'

18

RETAIL THERAPY

Mikey had been right. Market Furnley was an upmarket town with plenty of shops where Sasha could spend her money. It was a shame the girls weren't here for "spending spree number two". Grandpa Wilf had told her to spend, spend, spend, and that's what she was going to do. Retail therapy was just what she needed.

First stop was the designer sunglasses shop. Sasha tried on several pairs until she found the ones that suited her best. She wouldn't have been able to afford them before, but she could now! The next shop that caught her eye was a small boutique. The dresses were gorgeous, so she bought three. Chloe and Kerstin were going to love them. Sasha then stopped outside a bag shop. She peered in the window before pushing the door open. A new cross body bag for wearing in the countryside was a must. Well, it wasn't, but it helped shift more of the cash.

Sasha checked the time on her phone. She needed to catch the next bus if she wanted to return to the farm by four-thirty. There was just enough time to buy two bottles of champagne to celebrate Lawrie's move from the big city. Sasha climbed onto the bus armed with her purchases. She hadn't had time to buy wellies but guessed she could get some in the village. From her earlier bus trip, she estimated it was only a twenty minute walk from the farm, and with the weather being so nice, she looked forward to a leisurely stroll tomorrow.

It was four-fifteen when Sasha opened the door to the farmhouse. She climbed the stairs and offloaded her shopping in her room. Sasha hung the dresses in her wardrobe so they didn't crease and grabbed the bottles of champagne before going back down the stairs and strolling into the kitchen. Sasha felt hungry and was looking forward to a Chinese takeaway. She rummaged through the kitchen drawers to find the cutlery and opened all the cupboards in search of champagne glasses. Well, wine glasses would have done, but there were only tumblers. Sasha smiled. Next time she was in Market Furnley, she would buy the boys some decent glasses. Tumblers would have to do for tonight.

The sound of footsteps running down the stairs

made Sasha turn to see Mikey walking into the kitchen with wet hair. 'I've just had a quick shower before dinner. I thought I should make an effort with a lady in the house.'

Sasha laughed. 'There's no need to change your habits while I'm here.'

The slam of a car door alerted the pair to Lawrie's arrival. He walked into the kitchen carrying the takeaway meal. 'I've done it! I've finally left miserable Margaret behind and followed my dreams.'

Mikey held out his hand to shake his friend's. 'Welcome home, mate.'

Sasha popped a champagne cork and filled three tumblers. 'We should have a toast to Lawrie's happy ever after. I've worked in that call centre, and the farm is a far nicer environment.'

The trio clinked glasses, and Sasha couldn't resist asking, 'Did your mother get my resignation? I emailed it this morning.'

Lawrie gulped his champagne. 'She certainly did. I didn't tell her where either of us have gone. She won't be bothered. She was on the phone booking a couple of temps from tomorrow. At least I've flown the nest before her deadline. It feels good to have taken control of my life.'

Mikey bit into a duck spring roll, then wiped his mouth on a serviette before speaking to Lawrie, 'I can't tell you how much of a relief it is to have you here. The contractors are arriving on Wednesday, and they mentioned today they want an initial payment in cash before they start. I'll need to pop to the bank in the morning. Tomorrow's the open day for potential cafeteria managers, so it would be great if you could show everyone around and explain our plans. I won't be out for long.'

Lawrie smiled. 'I can do that. No problem.'

Sasha swallowed a mouthful of noodles before interrupting the conversation, 'I've got plenty of cash I can lend you. I brought my inheritance with me. It was the first thing I packed when I left London yesterday. It would help if you could spend the cash and pay it into my account later. There's no rush.'

Mikey could see Sasha's point. 'Thanks, Sasha. That saves me from going into town tomorrow; I can stay here and keep an eye on Lawrie. I don't want him choosing the prettiest girl who turns up to run the cafeteria. We need someone with business management skills, along with catering experience. The farm shop will be in the same building, so we'll need a special person to cope.'

Sasha raised her eyebrows. Well, that ruled *her* out. She chuckled to herself; why was she even thinking about a job on the farm? She was far more suited to living in London. She was only here as a stopgap while her short-lived fame subsided. Sasha was pleased to have been of use in loaning Mikey the cash. There must be something else she could do while she was here. Sasha's thoughts turned to the weekend and Adam's visit. She wondered if he would be bringing Chloe.

Mikey must have read her thoughts. 'Chloe and Kerstin are coming down at the weekend with Adam and Blake.'

Sasha was miffed she hadn't heard first. At least she would be able to give them their dresses. Buying wine glasses was now high on her agenda. 'Do you need me to do anything in preparation for our guests? Will they be staying over? I could change bedding, clean the house, and order food. Just let me know what's required.'

Lawrie glanced at Mikey before responding, 'You're not here as our servant, but as you have asked so nicely, we *could* do with some help on the housekeeping front. We're not used to having visitors. Do whatever you think's best, and we'll pay you for your time.'

Sasha waved an arm in the air. 'You don't have to pay me. *I* should be paying *you* for the accommodation. Leave it with me. The house will be shining like a new pin by the weekend.'

Mikey and Lawrie went to bed by nine-thirty, ready for an early start in the morning, allowing Sasha to familiarise herself with the farmhouse. The sofa would look so much better with new cushions; a new rug in the kitchen was a must; then there was the bed linen. Sasha hadn't seen inside Mikey and Lawrie's rooms, but she guessed their duvet sets had holes like the ones in the other bedrooms. Chloe and Kerstin wouldn't feel comfortable sleeping in holey sheets. Lawrie had told her to "do whatever she thought was best". Sasha felt quite excited about giving the dreary farmhouse a makeover.

Sasha tidied the kitchen, loaded the dishwasher and turned it on before heading to bed. She would sleep well tonight. Sasha was doing something worthwhile for the first time in a long time. She knew the situation was temporary, but it was just what she needed while she figured out what to do with the rest of her life. Sasha checked her phone. She'd messaged Adam earlier, but he hadn't responded. That was strange.

Sasha yawned and buried her face in her pillow while counting how many sets of bed linen she needed to buy tomorrow. There were seven bedrooms, but how many would they use at the weekend? Adam could share with her, Chloe could stay with Mikey, Kerstin and Blake could share, that just left Lawrie in his room. So, four bedrooms to clean and spruce up. That would be enough work on the bedrooms for one week. There was still the living area to clean before their guests arrived on Saturday. Flowers were a must for the hallway and dining table. Sasha yawned again, and within seconds, she was fast asleep.

19

MORE SHOPPING

There was no way Sasha could get back from Market Furnley to the farm on the bus with all her shopping, so she decided to take a taxi. Mikey and Lawrie were surprised to see the taxi pulling up in front of the farmhouse as they took six potential candidates for the cafeteria manager role on a guided tour of the premises. With the work on the new building not starting until tomorrow, they were killing time by showing people around the farm. This morning hadn't gone well. A few disgruntled members of the group didn't buy into the dreams of two young men who weren't old enough to run a farm, let alone a cafeteria and shop.

Sasha piled her shopping on the kitchen floor and put the kettle on. She was looking forward to a cup of tea and a ready-made sandwich she'd bought from the bakery in Market Furnley. Half an hour later, she was joined by the boys. Sasha smiled at them. 'How did it go this morning? Have you found the perfect person for your new venture?'

Lawrie dragged a chair out from under the table and sat down. 'I don't know what's wrong with people. I understand they can't see the new building yet in all its glory, but they weren't interested in hearing our plans. If I didn't know better, I'd think they'd all been paid to come here this morning to put a spanner in the works. They didn't have one good thing to say about our vision.'

Mikey sighed. 'I'm not surprised. Most of the locals are set in their ways. It will take time for them to adjust to the farm becoming a hub of the community.' Mikey stared at Sasha's empty plate. 'I see you've eaten. I'll rustle something up for us before we get back to work.'

Sasha stood up. 'Sit down, and *I'll* rustle something up. I bought filled rolls for you both and cakes from the bakery in Market Furnley.'

Mikey rubbed his hands together. 'Has anyone ever told you you're an angel?'

Sasha giggled. 'Yes. Oswald, remember?'

Lawrie stared at the pile of shopping. 'What have you bought this morning?'

'Nothing much. Just wine glasses, a mat, cushions and four sets of bedding.'

Lawrie's mouth fell open. 'Do we need all of that?'

Sasha poured mugs of tea. 'Yes, you do. You told me to "do whatever I thought was best".'

Lawrie glanced at Mikey. 'Are you OK with all of this?'

Mikey smiled. 'I'm more than OK. Thanks, Sasha. Just let us know how much you've spent so we can reimburse you.'

Sasha shook her head. 'There's no charge. It's the least I can do with everything you've done for me. Besides, you wouldn't need wine glasses and new bedding if my friends hadn't invited themselves to stay at the weekend.' Sasha glanced at the clock on the kitchen wall. 'Is that the time already? I should get a move on. I didn't get chance to buy any wellies yesterday, so I'll walk into the village. I need some cleaning products, too.' Sasha grabbed her new cross body bag and waved as she dashed out of the kitchen.

Mikey stared at Lawrie. 'Sasha's changed.'

Lawrie bit into his cheese and pickle roll as he nodded. He'd hoped that taking Sasha out of London would turn her into a country girl. He didn't expect her to transition so quickly. Adam was a city boy through

and through. Lawrie allowed himself a wry smile –
good things come to those who wait.

*

The village had just one shop, a pub and a church. A
sign "Furnley End" stood next to a bridge spanning the
river, which Sasha had followed down from the farm.

Sasha pushed the shop door open to the sound of
bells. She looked up in surprise. Before long, an elderly
lady ambled out of a room at the back of the shop.
'You must be Mikey's young lady. We've heard about
you.'

Sasha shut the door and glanced around at the
rotting fruit and sparse variety of vegetables on display.
The shop smelt musty, and the shiny black eyes that
bore into her made her feel very uncomfortable. Sasha
walked up to the formidable woman, whom she
instantly disliked. She'd get the wellies, then never set
foot in the shop again. 'My name's Sasha, what's
yours?'

'Moira.'

'Well, Moira. I'm only here on a quick visit. I need
a pair of wellies.'

'What size?'

'Four.'

Moira shook her head with a twinkle in her eyes. 'Well, you're out of luck. They start at eight.'

Sasha felt relieved. 'Thank you so much for your time, Moira. Oh, and just to set the record straight, I'm not Mikey's young lady.'

Sasha pulled the door open, which set the bells ringing again. She stepped outside and took a deep breath of fresh air to rid her lungs of the stench of such a morbid woman and her sinister abode. Sasha headed for the bus stop with a sigh. She'd have to go into Market Furnley for a second time today. It was the only place she'd have any chance of buying a pair of size four wellies.

*

With wellies purchased from the department store, along with cleaning products and two board games the friends could have fun with at the weekend, Sasha waited at the bus stop to return to the farm. The bus arrived, and Sasha climbed on. One person was already on the bus, and he waved to her. 'Come and sit beside me. I'm keen to know how Mikey's doing at the farm.'

Sasha was wary, but the young man looked presentable. He had curly brown hair, a warm smile, and the kindest brown eyes Sasha had ever seen. He also had good manners; he stood up to help Sasha with her bags. 'My name's Mark. You must be Sasha.'

Sasha shook Mark's hand. 'I'm surprised you know who I am.'

Mark smiled. 'Everyone knows everyone around here. The farm hands are always a source of information.' Mark tapped his nose. 'They don't all use the internet, though. I must be the only one who's seen your performances at St Pancras and the Wensley International Hotel. You're a very gifted musician.'

Sasha gasped. 'Have you told anyone about me?'

Mark shook his head. 'Of course not. I assumed your sudden appearance on the farm meant you needed to escape the bright lights of London. It's not my place to divulge your whereabouts.'

Sasha let out a sigh of relief. 'Thank you. It's a long story. All I can say is staying on the farm with Mikey and Lawrie is a refreshing change.'

'Ah, I see, Lawrie's finally made the move, has he?'

'Yes. He has.'

Mark turned to face Sasha. 'You were amazing with that little girl who interrupted your performance on Sunday. Have you ever thought of giving lessons?'

Sasha frowned. 'It's not something I had in mind.'

'Well, why don't you try it out for size? A seven-year-old boy in the village has potential, but his family can't afford a tutor. Little Tommy quite often pops into the vicarage to play the piano. I've been trying to help him, but I'm not very good at it.'

The vicarage! Sasha stared into Mark's kind brown eyes. He looked too young to be a vicar. Sasha stuttered, 'Well … well, I suppose I could help you.'

A smile lit up Mark's face. 'That would be great! Shall we say four o'clock tomorrow afternoon? I'm childminding Tommy after school until his grandmother shuts up shop. Moira always escapes her duties by four-forty-five. The locals are used to that.'

20

PIANO LESSON

Sasha walked along the riverbank from the farm to Furnley End. Mikey and Lawrie had found her accounts of her meetings with Moira, then Mark, and the impending piano lesson with little Tommy hilarious. They said the vicarage was the big house behind the church, so it would be easy for Sasha to find.

Sasha had kept herself busy all morning cleaning the upstairs rooms. She'd made lunch for everyone and taken two rounds of tea and coffee outside for the contractors who'd turned up today to start the building work. Keeping busy had taken her mind off the prospect of bumping into morbid Moira when she collected her grandson later this afternoon.

It was three-forty-five when Sasha pulled on the roped doorbell of the vicarage. She couldn't help a little chuckle. Another bell! She hadn't planned on taking up bell-ringing this week. Mark opened the door wearing jeans and a white T-shirt. He was carrying a dumbbell. 'Hi, Sasha. You've caught me doing my workout. Come on through to the kitchen, and I'll make a cuppa before Tommy arrives.'

From first impressions, the vicarage was spotless. Sasha asked, 'Do you have a cleaner?'

Mark nodded. 'I certainly do. I couldn't manage without Sharon coming in once a week. She's got a nice little business going. I recommended her to Mikey's father, but he said there was no place for cleaners on farms.' Mark rubbed his chin. 'Now, there's a thought: Mikey and Lawrie may be keen to use Sharon's services. You could mention it to them. You'll meet her in a moment. She picks Tommy up from school and drops him off here on Wednesdays.'

Right on cue, the doorbell rang, and Mark paced down the hallway to answer it. 'Hello you two. Come inside and meet Sasha. She's a brilliant pianist and is looking forward to teaching Tommy a thing or two today.'

Sharon was stunning. She had long, black, shiny hair piled on top of her head, and her makeup was immaculate. Her black twinkling eyes were framed by long lashes that were too natural to be false. She held out her professionally manicured hand to shake Sasha's. 'Hi, Sasha. Mark's been singing your praises. It's very good of you to give Tommy a free piano lesson this afternoon. I must dash now, or I'll be late for my next client. Mum will collect Tommy as soon as she closes the shop.'

Mark stepped outside with Sharon, leaving Tommy standing before Sasha with his black eyes narrowed. 'My Granny doesn't like you.'

Sasha locked eyes with the little boy. 'Well, *I* don't like your Granny. Mark is nice, though, and we need to look like we're getting along for his sake. Now, come with me; I'll try not to make the lesson too painful for you. Show me what you already know, and we'll take it from there.'

At four-forty-eight, the vicarage doorbell rang again. This time, Tommy jumped off the piano stool and ran to the front door to meet his grandmother. Moira didn't venture inside. Mark waved the pair off before closing the door and searching for Sasha, who was still in the drawing room, standing beside the piano.

Mark raised his eyebrows. 'How did it go?'

Sasha held her shoulders back. 'Tommy has potential. I've asked him to consider what he learnt today, and if he thinks it worthwhile, we can have another lesson next week.'

Mark was surprised. 'Next week? Will you still be here then?'

Sasha nodded. 'I need to stay another week to sort my life out. With the mess it's in, it'll take at least another week.'

Mark's eyes widened. 'Would you like to tell me about it? I'm a good listener.'

Sasha felt drawn to Mark. He undoubtedly had all the qualities of an excellent vicar. Speaking to an impartial outsider could be just what Sasha needed to give her clarity on how to move forward with her life.

With the conversation flowing for over an hour and Sasha nowhere near finished with pouring out her thoughts and feelings, she messaged Lawrie:

> *I'm still at the vicarage. I made a lasagne earlier. It's in the fridge. It needs to go in the oven at 180 degrees. Please eat without me. I'm not sure what time I'll be home. Sasha x*

It was after seven o'clock when Sasha finally came up for air. Mark was pleased she was able to confide in him so deeply. He wasn't surprised about the locals being against Mikey and Lawrie's plans for the farm or the fact that Moira had been less than welcoming. Mark could help Sasha resolve that situation; he was sure of it. The way she'd been speaking about her family, friends and career gave him the feeling that, just by compartmentalising her thoughts, Sasha would find the best solutions for her.

Mark was ravenous. 'Shall we have a break? Fancy chicken fajitas? I'm certainly in need of sustenance.'

Sasha's stomach was rumbling. 'Are you cooking?'

'If you're willing to take the risk.'

Sasha laughed. 'OK then. Can I help?'

'There's a bottle of homemade wine in the fridge. One of the parishioners gave it to me on Sunday. You could open that and taste it before you pour me a glass. If it's a bit dubious, open a bottle of whatever you fancy from the cellar.'

'You have a cellar?'

Mark smiled. 'I certainly do. It came as part of the job. Well, part of the vicarage, but I make good use of it.'

*

Back at the farmhouse, Lawrie was perturbed. He loaded the dishwasher as he wrestled with his thoughts. Mark was a very eligible bachelor; he was intelligent and handsome, lived in a large house with no mortgage, and even had a piano! It had been wrong to laugh about Sasha's chance meeting with him. Mark was a threat.

Mikey's phone rang, and he waved it in the air to attract Lawrie's attention. 'Adam's calling. I'll see what he wants.'

Lawrie stood rooted to the spot as Mikey took the call, 'Hi, Adam. How are things in London? … What? You can't get hold of Sasha, and she needs to know you can't make it at the weekend.'

Lawrie's ears pricked up. He mouthed a word to Mikey, 'Why?'

Mikey nodded before responding to Adam, 'Why can't you make it at the weekend? … Oh, I see … I'm sure Sasha will understand … Thanks for letting us know, bro.'

Mikey ended the call and advised Lawrie of the reason for Adam's absence, 'He forgot it's the Rugby Club Presentation Evening on Saturday night.'

Lawrie raised his eyebrows. 'But Blake's still coming; and he's in the same team.'

Mikey raised his hands in the air. 'It's nothing to do with us. Do you want to let Sasha know, or shall I?'

Lawrie tried not to smile. 'You do it.'

21

INSIDE INFORMATION

Sasha was up bright and early. She couldn't wait to share her news with Lawrie and Mikey. It had been a late night at the vicarage, and the farmhouse was in darkness when Mark walked Sasha home. This time, it was the boys who woke to the smell of bacon coming from the kitchen.

Lawrie and Mikey ate their breakfasts as Sasha divulged her findings, 'Moira is the nucleus of your downfall. She's poisoning the minds of the locals against your plans. When your cafeteria and farm shop are up and running, she'll be out of a job.'

Mikey pierced a sausage. 'That's obvious.'

Sasha continued, 'So the best way to get the

community's buy-in is to offer Moira a position at the "new place to be" in Furnley End.'

Mikey swallowed his tea. 'She won't be welcome here.'

Sasha shook her head. 'That's not the way to view it – we need to be creative and turn the negative into a positive.'

Mikey raised an eyebrow at Lawrie. They should have known it; Mark had given Sasha the stupid idea about recruiting the village's most obnoxious resident. The vicar may see the good in everyone, but Moira couldn't be saved from her sins. She should be avoided at all costs.

Sasha was bubbly despite her late night; she was full of ideas, 'Another good way to get buy-in from the locals is to sell their produce in the farm shop. There are some talented people in the village: knitters, jam makers, and wine producers. The list is endless!'

Lawrie sat back in his chair. That didn't sound like a bad idea. He stared at Sasha. 'Did Mark have any other suggestions?'

Sasha blushed. 'Yes, he did. He said the wider community needed a piano teacher. We spent ages searching online last night, and the nearest one is thirty miles away. Mark says we'd be onto a winner if we incorporated piano lessons into our new venture.'

Lawrie stared at Mikey, who raised an eyebrow before speaking, 'That isn't a bad idea.'

Lawrie's mind was working overtime, and his heart was pounding. Sasha had mentioned "our new venture". Was she planning on staying at the farm? If Mikey agreed about the piano part, then Sasha would never go back to London. She'd have everything she needed right here.

Mikey pushed his chair back and stood up while trying not to smile. 'I'm easy about the piano suggestion. Why don't you two mull it over while I pop out to check on the contractors? They're arriving in their droves today.'

Sasha sat down next to Lawrie. 'What do you think? Would the piano part fit in with your vision for the farm? Would you mind me staying on here to help?'

Lawrie's blue eyes twinkled, and his trademark cheeky grin lit up his face. 'I think I could cope with that. You've brought many ideas to the table, including the name of our new venture.'

'The name?'

Lawrie nodded. 'Yes. Mikey's left that up to me and, up until now, I'd drawn a blank.'

'What name did I suggest?'

The New Place to Be.' Sasha giggled, and Lawrie

continued, 'I can just see it now: *The New Place to Be* – Cafeteria, Farm Shop, Community Allotment, Seasonal Events, Bed & Breakfast, Glamping Huts, Resident Piano Tutor … the list is endless.'

Sasha gasped. 'That's a good idea about Bed & Breakfast and Glamping Huts.'

Lawrie blushed. 'I was getting carried away there. But with you on board, the possibilities are endless.'

Sasha laughed. She hadn't felt so happy in years. Lawrie's thoughts turned to Adam and his phone call yesterday. Mikey hadn't yet had the chance to pass on his message to Sasha. Lawrie didn't want to upset her while she was so upbeat. 'I'd best get a move on. Mikey's got his hands full out there.'

Sasha picked up the empty plates. 'I need to get a move on too. I'm behind with the cleaning. I'm so excited that everyone's coming down from London at the weekend. I can't wait to tell them how well things are working out here. No one would have guessed I'd feel at home on a farm.'

Lawrie felt like punching the air but refrained from doing so. Sasha was making her own decisions and doing very well in the process. Things were taking off, and Lawrie couldn't be happier with how events were unfolding.

*

It had been a busy day for everyone, and as Sasha headed for bed, Mikey remembered Adam's call, 'Oh, Sasha, I've been meaning to tell you, Adam called yesterday. He can't make it at the weekend as it's the Rugby Club's Presentation Evening. He forgot. He sends his apologies.'

Sasha was deep in thought as she climbed the stairs. Adam hadn't contacted her directly since she'd left London. In her heart of hearts, she knew he wasn't the country type. He couldn't even face coming down for a weekend. Blake had chosen to come to the farm with Kerstin instead of attending a rugby club event. The realisation then hit Sasha that she wasn't upset about Adam letting her down. If anything, she was pleased to have the chance to rebuild her life without anyone else to worry about.

Sasha sent Adam a message:

> *Hi, Adam. We both know it's not working. Let's call it a day. Have fun at the Rugby Club Presentation Event. Also, please thank your grandfather for the job offer, but I won't be returning to London for a while. It was very kind of him. Take care, Sasha.*

Adam messaged straight back:

Hi, Sasha. You know me too well. I'm a city boy at heart. My grandfather will be disappointed, but at least I have him back now. So, thank you for that. I hope things continue to work out well for you. Don't overlook Lawrie – he's a good guy. Wishing you all the best. Adam

Sasha sighed in relief as she turned off her bedside light. She felt at peace. Strangely, Mark had said the same thing about Lawrie yesterday. Tonight, Sasha didn't close her eyes, counting the number of duvets that needed replacing. Instead, she couldn't wipe away the sight of the cheeky grin she had first encountered in Margaret's office at the call centre. Sometimes, what someone has been looking for has been there all along.

22

SURPRISE GUESTS

Friday was busier than Sasha had planned. Their friends decided to travel to the farm after work so they could stay for two nights rather than one. Mikey and Lawrie had taken the news in their stride, but Sasha was planning to finish the cleaning and change the sheets on Friday evening. She'd washed all the new ones and had been cleaning and airing the rooms before making up the beds.

Mikey placed an arm around her shoulders. 'Lawrie and I will finish early, and after we've showered and changed, we'll help you with the last-minute jobs. Just tell us what you need us to do. The house is looking amazing, by the way. I can't remember the last time we had fresh flowers. They make such a difference.' Mikey kissed Sasha's cheek. 'We're pleased you're here. You've been a Godsend.'

Sasha blushed. 'Not an angel?'

Mikey laughed. 'Same thing. Oh, and don't worry about buying food for dinner tonight. We'll walk into the village. The pub does meals.'

*

By seven o'clock, the friends were ready to welcome their guests. Blake was driving Kerstin and Chloe to the farm, so it was somewhat of a surprise when a two-seater convertible BMW sped up the driveway before tooting its horn. Sasha winced. 'It's Oswald and Rafferty. Did they say they were coming?' Lawrie and Mikey shook their heads before going outside to greet their visitors.

Oswald was as effervescent as usual. 'Surprise, surprise! We couldn't resist joining you when we heard you were having a little soiree this weekend.'

Sasha rushed outside and grabbed Lawrie's arm before whispering, 'I only cleaned four bedrooms.'

Lawrie whispered back, 'They can have my room. I don't mind sleeping in one of the others; I've got used to holey sheets.'

Sasha cringed. 'The sheets aren't holey anymore. I've thrown them away, along with the duvets and pillows. The bedding in the other three rooms smelt worse than Moira's shop. I've been leaving the windows open to air them.'

Lawrie could sense Sasha's panic. 'Don't worry. I'll sleep on the sofa. It'll be comfy now you've bought those nice new cushions. I'll pop upstairs and move my things before they come inside.'

Ten minutes later, Blake's Volkswagen Golf crunched up the gravel drive, and Sasha ran to hug her friends as they climbed out of the car. 'I'm so pleased to see you both!'

Kerstin raised an eyebrow. 'I suppose you've heard Adam can't make it.'

Chloe clung to Sasha's arm. 'We hope you're not upset about that.'

Sasha shrugged her shoulders. 'I'm not bothered at all. I ended things with Adam yesterday. I came to the realisation that he's not my type.'

Lawrie stood rooted to the spot. He'd just run out of the house. Had he heard Sasha correctly? He glanced over at Mikey, who winked and did a thumbs-up sign. Lawrie couldn't contain his delight. He walked over to hug Kerstin and Chloe and shake hands with Blake. 'It's great to see you all. We can't wait to show you around and tell you our plans. Things are taking off at a pace. Sasha's been a star this week, a real Godsend!'

Mikey chuckled. Lawrie couldn't keep his cheeky grin off his face. 'I agree. Sasha's been an angel in disguise.'

Kerstin and Chloe frowned at one another, and Oswald did a little clap. 'I was the first to notice Sasha's star potential. She's an Angel from Heaven.'

Sasha blushed as she directed her gaze at Oswald. 'Less of that. Also, no filming is allowed this weekend. I just want a quiet life.'

Lawrie couldn't resist squeezing Sasha as he smiled at their friends. 'Sasha's going to stay at the farm and teach the piano. We're thrilled, aren't we, Mikey?'

Kerstin and Chloe raised their eyebrows while waiting for Mikey's response, 'We certainly are.'

Chloe whispered to Kerstin, 'We'll need to find another flatmate.'

Kerstin whispered back, 'You'll need to find two. Blake's asked me to move in with him.'

Chloe's heart sank. Both of her friends were deserting her. They'd always been a team, and now she was left on her own. Why couldn't *she* have a happy ending? Life was not fair.

Mikey picked up Chloe's case. 'How long are you staying for? This case is heavy.'

Chloe gasped. 'Be careful with that. I brought some more of Sasha's things with me. Her inheritance is in there. Blake got it working.'

Mikey smiled. 'Sasha will be delighted the cuckoo's found its voice. Let's take it up to our room. We can break the news to her later.'

Chloe's eyes widened. 'Our room?'

'Yes. Sasha didn't think you'd mind, and I'm not complaining. It saved her from having to clean an extra bedroom. She's worked like a trojan this week.'

Chloe followed Mikey into the farmhouse and up the stairs. Sasha had made herself at home here. Chloe tried to ignore a pang of jealousy. Less than a week ago, Chloe had told Sasha *she* wanted to live on the farm. Now, Sasha was living Chloe's dream.

Sasha was preparing pre-dinner drinks and nibbles in the kitchen when she felt a hand on the small of her back. Lawrie was leaning over her shoulder. 'You smell amazing … I meant those sausage rolls smell great. Homemade ones straight out of the oven are always the best.'

Sasha frowned when Lawrie picked one up and bit into it. Was she being delusional? Happy-go-lucky Lawrie wouldn't notice her perfume. That was more of an Adam comment. Too much time with the vicar had scrambled her mind. Still, she had to keep focused. The news that Chloe would be alone in the apartment in London meant Sasha needed to get a plan in place sooner rather than later. The girls had been there for Sasha when she needed them, and now it was Chloe's turn to receive some help.

23

DINNER AT THE PUB

The friends walked along the riverbank to the village pub. Sasha linked her arm through Chloe's. 'Do you still want to live on the farm?'

Chloe looked over her shoulder to see if anyone was in earshot. 'Even more so now that *you've* moved in. How could we make it work?'

Sasha tapped her nose. 'Quite easily. You've got a degree in Business Management, *and* you worked in the cafeteria at university for three years. You've got everything the boys need.'

Mikey glanced at Lawrie. 'You *do* realise Sharon still works in the pub on Fridays?'

Lawrie sighed. 'Does she? I could have done without that.'

Oswald and Rafferty took in the sights as they strolled into the village, which was quaint and untouched by time. This was their first visit to the farm, and they were sure it wouldn't be their last. How wonderful to have friends in the countryside. Furnley End was the perfect weekend retreat. Once Mikey & Lawrie's vision was off the ground, Oswald would happily promote *The New Place to Be* on social media to his thousands of followers.

Kerstin smiled at Blake. 'Why didn't you stay in London this weekend with Adam? Weren't you in line for an award at the Rugby Club Presentation Evening?'

Blake's large, soft hand squeezed Kerstin's. 'I'm Player of the Season. Adam's going to accept the award on my behalf. And in answer to your first question, I'd much rather spend a weekend away with you than at some boozy event at the rugby club. Besides, I want to see Sasha's face when she hears the cuckoo clock.'

Kerstin squeezed Adam's hand back before laughing. It was only two weeks ago that Sasha had received the cash from Grandpa Wilf. The changes to the girls' lives since then had been dramatic. Kerstin would be forever grateful to Sasha's grandfather. He'd led her to Blake. She was excited about moving in with the gentle giant. For the first time in her life, Kerstin was convinced she'd found "the one".

Mikey pushed the pub door open for his friends to

walk through. Oswald glanced around. 'Charming, absolutely charming.'

Rafferty walked up to the bar. 'I'm impressed you have a selection of real ales. Which one would you recommend?'

Sharon stared over Rafferty's shoulder. Was that Lawrie who'd just sat down with a group of girls? She didn't like the look of that. Rafferty was still waiting for an answer. Sharon poured a pint before handing it to him. 'This one's a good one.'

Rafferty took hold of his pint, and Mikey walked over to speak to Sharon. 'Please put our drinks on a tab. We'll be eating here, too. We'll settle up at the end. It's great for Lawrie and me to have our girlfriends here this weekend.'

As anticipated, Sharon's face dropped. The pub door opened at that point, and the ever-smiling Mark walked through. He waved to Sharon before acknowledging the other members of the parish who were socialising on a Friday night. Mikey whispered to her, 'Don't go misbehaving with the vicar. I've seen the way he looks at you.'

Sharon blushed, and Mikey turned away with a chuckle. Mark was big enough to fight off any advances from needy Sharon. At least she'd keep her claws out of Lawrie tonight. Mikey didn't want anything

146

disrupting the budding relationship between Sasha and his best friend. He just wished Lawrie would seal the deal and stop pussyfooting around.

During the meal, Sasha began to drop hints to help Chloe. 'You're wasted in London with your degree in Business Management.'

Kerstin raised an eyebrow. 'No, she's not. She's got a great job at a very respectable firm. Chloe earns more than me.'

Sasha left it a few minutes, then tried another tactic. 'The experience Chloe gained at university from working in the cafeteria has set her in good stead to choose any career she wants.'

Lawrie frowned. Had Sasha had too much to drink? She was coming up with some random comments. Mikey blushed, he knew what Sasha was trying to do, but it only made things worse. Chloe would never leave a high-powered job in London to work on a farm. They couldn't afford her for a start.

Blake's eyes twinkled. He could see the chemistry between Mikey and Chloe, so he offered an outsider's advice, 'Has anyone asked Chloe what she would like to do? It sounds to me there's a job for her on the farm if she wants it.'

Mikey blushed, 'The cafeteria and farm shop won't be up and running for at least another twelve weeks.'

Chloe took her chance. 'That's perfect! I need to give twelve weeks' notice to leave my job. It must be fate. I'll resign on Monday – that's if you'll have me here, of course.'

Lawrie grinned at Mikey, who was unsure about the situation. 'We'll pay you a salary, but it won't be the same as what you're on now.'

Chloe smiled. 'I won't need the salary I'm on now if I'm not living in London. Please take a chance on me. I can't bear to live in a different part of the country to Sasha.'

Kerstin narrowed her eyes at that comment but could see the benefit to all parties concerned. At least she wouldn't feel guilty now about moving in with Blake.

Mikey stared at Lawrie, who winked his agreement. 'Well, it looks like we have a new employee. Let's have a toast to *The New Place to Be's* Business Manager.'

Sasha noticed Sharon glaring at the group from behind the bar. She chuckled before making a tongue-in-cheek comment, 'Chloe will no doubt need help in the shop. Moira's very experienced, but I doubt she'd be interested in working at the farm.'

Mikey and Lawrie looked daggers at Sasha, who felt pleased she'd sewn a seed to stop morbid Moira from scuppering their plans. They didn't *have* to give her a job. It may just give her food for thought so she conformed going forward.

*

It was one o'clock in the morning when the guests finally took to their beds. Sasha's head was spinning; there was no way she would get to sleep tonight. Chloe would be joining them on the farm, and that brought endless possibilities. Then, there was the piano tutor role for her. Sasha needed two things before she could start: A piano and a qualification. She'd already searched online and found a piano teacher's course. It wasn't cheap, but she had enough money in her bank account to pay for it. A second-hand piano would be an excellent way to spend more cash. Sasha couldn't believe how quickly she was managing to spend ten thousand pounds.

There were only two loose ends in her mind now: Grandpa Wilf and her father. She hadn't told either of them where she'd disappeared to. Her mother wouldn't be bothered, but Sasha was wary of her father coming to find her. She also missed her regular chats with Grandpa Wilf. She was surprised he hadn't contacted her all week.

Sasha wished she'd brought a glass of water up to bed. She usually did, but tonight had been chaotic when everyone went upstairs. It was quiet now, so Sasha climbed out of bed and crept down the stairs on her way to the kitchen. A light was on in the living room, and she peered inside. 'Oh, sorry, Lawrie. I forgot you're sleeping on the sofa.'

Lawrie held out an arm. 'Come over here and tell me how you managed to turn things around so quickly. You've been at the farm less than a week, and now we have a piano tutor, a business manager and a farmhouse that has never been so homely. We also have a name for our new venture and the prospect of Moira knocking on our door first thing in the morning asking for a job.'

Sasha giggled as she sat on the sofa next to Lawrie. 'Am I too pushy?'

Lawrie's eyes twinkled. 'You could say that. But I like it.'

Sasha thumped his shoulder. 'I can't sleep tonight with everything that's going on.'

Lawrie stared into her eyes. 'Me neither. Why don't we have a cuddle? I don't know about you, but I could do with one.'

Sasha rested her head on Lawrie's shoulder, and he stroked her hair. 'This feels nice. I could nod off if we stay like this for a while.'

Sasha closed her eyes. 'Me too.'

24

AN EARLY START

The following morning, the farmhouse doorbell rang at seven-thirty. Mikey jumped out of bed and grabbed his dressing gown. He'd been looking forward to a lie-in. The farm hands were putting in extra shifts this weekend so that Lawrie and Mikey could spend time with their guests.

Mikey opened the door to the sight of Moira holding a gingham-covered basket. His mouth dropped open when she handed it to him with a smile. 'I was up early this morning, so I made scones for you and your guests. They're still warm.'

Moira turned and waved before climbing into her Mini Cooper. She tooted as she sped down the drive. After waking from a deep sleep, Sasha and Lawrie peered through the living room window. Lawrie ran his hands through his dark-blonde hair before yawning, 'That's Moira's car.'

Sasha dashed into the kitchen before Mikey entered the living room. He held the basket aloft for Lawrie to see. 'A miracle has happened. Moira has made scones for us all, *and* she was smiling.'

Lawrie could still feel Sasha's warmth. It had been the best night's sleep he'd ever had. She smelt terrific, and her hair was so soft. Mikey interrupted his tired friend. 'I know it's early, sleepyhead, but you need to take this all in. Moira may be the key to getting the villagers' buy-in to our plans.'

Lawrie stretched his arms while stifling another yawn. 'Sasha already mentioned that.'

Mikey frowned. 'Well, if Moira's scones are better than the ones from the bakery in Market Furnley, we should give serious thought to using her services.'

Sasha giggled from her position outside the living room door. She had a stiff neck from spending the night on the sofa, but she wasn't complaining. Lawrie was a good cuddler; he smelt great, *and* he didn't snore. Sasha smiled to herself; Lawrie was ticking lots of boxes.

Sasha climbed the stairs to get changed and bumped into Blake and Kerstin on their way down. Kerstin raised an eyebrow. 'Did you sleep downstairs last night?'

Sasha shook her head while lowering her eyes. 'Moira woke me up. I wondered what was going on, so I popped downstairs for a glass of water. I forgot to take one up with me last night. Mikey was the first to run downstairs to open the door. He's in the living room with Lawrie. Did the doorbell wake you both up, too?'

Blake gave a dimpled smile. 'We've been awake for ages. Sleeping through the sound of a cockerel is difficult when you're not used to it. It's certainly a different way of life in the country. It suits *you*, though. You're glowing.'

Sasha touched her cheek. 'It's all the fresh air and exercise. Anyway, I'll get dressed, then I can help Mikey with the breakfasts.'

Mikey ran past Sasha on the stairs. 'Thanks, Sasha. I need to get dressed, too. Apologies for the early wake-up call, guys. Let's hope Moira's scones are worth the disturbance.'

Lawrie was pulling on his jeans and T-shirt when Kerstin poked her head around the living room door. 'How did you get on sleeping on the sofa? It was very good of you to give up your room for Oswald and Rafferty.'

Lawrie gave a cheeky grin. 'I've never slept better.

I'll pop upstairs for a quick shower if one of the bathrooms is free.'

Blake winked at Kerstin, who winked back. No wonder Sasha was glowing.

*

There was a cheerful atmosphere around the breakfast table. The news of Moira's scones brought much debate and amusement. There would be pros and cons to be considered before employing her. Still, the signs were promising. Moira may not be too bad after all.

Sasha's phone rang. 'Excuse me, everyone, but I need to take this. My mother never calls me. Something must be up.' Sasha headed outside to take the call. 'Mum, what's wrong?'

'The care home just called. Your grandfather's gone missing. On top of that, your father's turned up. He's at the care home now and asking for your address in London. Can I give it to him? He's very persistent.'

Sasha shook her head as she raised her voice, 'No! Do not give him my address. What's he doing in Durham?'

'He came to visit your grandfather. That's how we've found out he's gone missing. He hasn't been seen since yesterday lunchtime.'

Sasha pulled at her hair. 'What can we do?!'

Angela didn't sound too bothered. 'We can't do anything, Sasha. The care home said he'll turn up when he's hungry.'

Sasha's heart was pounding. 'Has anyone tried to phone him?'

'He hasn't got his phone with him. It's still in his kitchen. Don't worry; he won't have gone far. I'll let you know when I hear anything. I'll be at the hairdressers this afternoon; but I'll be home later.'

Sasha walked back into the kitchen and slumped down on a chair. Chloe rushed over to hold her friend's hand. 'What's happened?'

'Grandpa Wilf's gone missing.'

The friends were absorbing the shocking news when Sasha's phone rang again. This time it was Adam. 'Adam! I've just had the most terrible news. Grandpa Wilf's gone missing.'

Adam could sense Sasha's panic down the phone. 'That's why I'm calling. Your grandfather's here with me. He's eating his breakfast. I just wanted to let you know he's safe.'

All eyes were on stalks as the friends tried to listen to the conversation. Sasha let out a sigh of relief. 'Where are you? Are you in your new apartment yet?'

'No. I'm still at the Wensley. Your grandfather

arrived last night. He'd caught a train from Durham and went to your apartment, but you're all down on the farm. Wilf had an old envelope in his pocket with the name of this hotel, so he came here instead. Anyway, he's been chatting to my grandfather this morning, and it soon became clear that Wilf's famous piano-playing granddaughter is you.'

Sasha blushed. 'Thanks for the call, Adam. Tell Grandpa Wilf to stay there. I'll come to London now if someone will give me a lift.' There were nods and thumbs up around the table.

Adam had more news for Sasha, 'Don't come to London. From what my grandfather has gathered, Wilf is running away from Ted. It's something to do with the ten thousand pounds. Stay on the farm, and I'll drive your grandfather down this morning. That way, Ted won't know where either of you are.'

25

SAFE HAVEN

The friends left Sasha and her grandfather alone in the kitchen. Grandpa Wilf's eyes darted around the place. 'Well, I'd never have guessed you'd end up living on a farm. Why didn't you send me your new address?'

Sasha was becoming impatient. 'Stop asking about me and tell me about *you*. Why are you running away from my father?'

Blake knocked on the kitchen door before entering. Grandpa Wilf was shocked to see him. 'Blake! What are *you* doing here?'

Blake handed Grandpa Wilf a crumpled piece of paper. 'I found this inside the cuckoo clock when I took the back off.'

Grandpa Wilf scratched his head. 'Well, I never. My wife must have hidden it in there. I threw it in the bin.'

Blake held out his hand to shake Grandpa Wilf's. 'Thanks for not informing on my grandfather. No wonder the clock wasn't working.'

Blake smiled at Sasha as he left the kitchen. Sasha grabbed hold of the piece of paper. 'Let me see that.'

The note read:

> *To the Neighbours at the bottom of my garden.*
>
> *Keep your noses out of my business. The package should not have been left with a neighbour. And YOU shouldn't have opened it. Keep schtum or else. YOU HAVE BEEN WARNED.*

Sasha's hand was shaking as she folded the note in half. 'Rupert was a drug dealer, wasn't he?' Grandpa Wilf nodded. 'How did my father get involved with all of this?'

Grandpa Wilf took a deep breath. 'Your father was a customer of Rupert's. He knows I turned a blind eye to their activities. When I moved into the care home, I took delivery of a parcel for Rupert from a courier. I had to sign for it. I noticed your father's scrawly handwriting on the label and looked inside.'

Sasha held her head in her hands. 'It was the ten thousand pounds, wasn't it?'

Grandpa Wilf nodded. 'Rupert was taken to hospital shortly after that. That's when I spotted an opportunity for you to receive an inheritance from your father. It won't be fair to you when he leaves all his money to his other children.'

Sasha frowned. 'Other children?'

'Yes. He's fathered two boys and a girl over the last seven years. He seems quite content with his latest wife.'

Sasha shuddered. So "once bitten, twice shy" was a lie, too.

Grandpa Wilf reached out to hold Sasha's hand, 'So, now you know why I needed you to spend the cash quickly. I wanted it gone before your father came looking for it. Now he's after me. If I hadn't signed for that package, Ted would never have known I was in the picture.'

There was another knock on the kitchen door. This time, Adam walked in. 'Blake's briefed us on Rupert's activities, and we couldn't help but hear about your father's involvement.' Sasha could see her friends huddled in the hallway. 'Can we come in and get our heads together about the best way forward?'

*

By two o'clock, a plan was in place. Adam waved as he sped down the drive on his way back to London, and Grandpa Wilf climbed the stairs to Sasha's room. 'Are you sure you don't mind me staying in your room tonight?'

Sasha smiled. 'Of course not. You're staying here until we can get you back safely to the care home.'

'Have you told them where I am? Does Angela know?'

'Not yet. We need to make sure my father's on a train back to London before we let everyone in Durham know you're safe.'

'Do you think Mr Wensley will be able to sort everything out?'

'I'm certain of it. Mr Wensley knows people in high places. My father won't be bothering either of us again.'

*

Ted ran to catch the four o'clock train. Finding Wilf would have to wait. Mr Wensley had messaged requesting a personal chat at his hotel this evening.

He'd said it would be to Ted's advantage. A chauffeur would collect him at Kings Cross station. Ted jumped into the first-class carriage that Mr Wensley had booked. For once in his life, Ted was rubbing shoulders with the best. Very Important Person sprang to mind. Yes – Ted was finally a VIP.

*

Sasha's phone rang. 'It's Adam, I'm back at the hotel. We've had confirmation your father's on the train. My grandfather will deal with things from here. Your worries are over, Sasha. The money's yours. You can spend it with a clear conscience. Oh, and by the way, I had to do a deal with my grandfather to get him to help us.'

'A deal? What sort of a deal?'

'I mentioned you were looking for a second-hand piano, so he's sending my grandmother's to the farm. He doesn't want anything for it. He just wants it to go to a good home.'

Sasha was embarrassed. 'I can't possibly accept a grand piano.'

Adam laughed. 'Oh, yes, you can. I'll not be having you upset my grandfather with all the help he's given to you and Wilf.' Adam ended the call. He was looking forward to a few beers tonight at the rugby club. Trust Blake to get Player of the Season. Adam smiled to himself. Blake wouldn't be as committed to the team in the future, not now he was going out with Kerstin. Adam would be in with a chance next year.

*

It had been an eventful day, and with the late night yesterday and early start this morning, everyone had retired to their beds before ten o'clock. Sasha curled up with Lawrie on the sofa before staring into his eyes. 'Those scones were delicious. We have a star baker in our midst. Have you changed your mind yet about giving Moira a job?'

Lawrie didn't get a chance to answer before the sound of a cuckoo startled the pair, making them jump off the sofa. After searching the living room, Sasha's inheritance was found in the sideboard. The sound of giggles from the hallway and feet running up the stairs gave the culprits away.

Sasha held the clock aloft. 'How do we stop this thing? It will be going all night. It's just cuckooed ten times. Next, it will be eleven, then twelve!'

Lawrie took the clock from her and crept up the stairs before placing it outside Kerstin and Blake's room. Lawrie returned to the living room with a grin on his face. He winked as he jumped onto the sofa, pulling Sasha into his arms. 'The clock specialist will soon put a stop to it.'

Sasha giggled as Lawrie pulled her closer, lifting her face to meet his. She closed her eyes as Lawrie's lips brushed against hers. Their first kiss didn't disappoint – far from it! That was another box ticked. Sasha couldn't find fault with kind, thoughtful, cheeky Lawrie. Sasha smiled to herself; there was a good chance she may have found "the one".

26

SUNDAY MORNING

Blake carried Kerstin and Chloe's luggage down the stairs. The trio needed to leave before lunch to take Grandpa Wilf to Kings Cross station. Angela had been briefed to meet her father when he arrived back in Durham at four o'clock.

Grandpa Wilf hugged Sasha. 'Now, do as you're told and keep spending the cash. Promise me that, pet.'

Sasha hugged her grandfather back. 'I promise. I wish you could have stayed for longer.'

Grandpa Wilf's eyes twinkled. 'I'm sure I'll pop down again to see you at some point. I'm looking forward to getting back to the care home today. It's quiz night on Sundays.'

Sasha's eyes glistened. 'Don't let Mum complain

about you running away.'

Grandpa Wilf winked. 'Running away? I was only off on a little trip to see my favourite granddaughter. Surely that's allowed at my age?'

Grandpa Wilf climbed into Blake's Volkswagen Golf, and Sasha hugged Kerstin and Chloe. 'Don't leave me down here alone for too long. Promise me you'll come back soon.'

Kerstin winked. 'Blake and I will be coming for free weekends away on a regular basis.'

Chloe smiled. 'I'll be back every weekend before I move to the farm for good. There's so much we need to do here!'

Oswald and Rafferty waved to the passing car as they walked up the drive on their return from a morning stroll. Oswald handed Sasha a hand-painted vase, and Rafferty gave Mikey an embroidered tea towel before reaching into his pocket and pulling out a pair of earrings, which he passed to Lawrie.

Oswald chuckled. 'The lovely Moira sent these for you. She's quite crafty. She's been selling lots of things she makes online. We believe that's why her shop's gone to pot. She's out the back doing the things she enjoys.'

Sasha's phone rang. She wondered why Adam was

calling her. 'Hi Adam … Oh, Mr Wensley! … I'm very well, thank you … What? …You're leaving to come to the farm now? … Yes … We're here all day … We look forward to seeing you soon.'

The friends were silent until Lawrie asked, 'Why's Mr Wensley on his way to the farm?'

Sasha blushed. 'Because he wants to ensure his wife's piano arrives safely. He also has a proposition to make after seeing Oswald's latest video.'

Rafferty frowned at Oswald. 'I said you shouldn't send it without speaking to Mikey and Lawrie.'

Oswald shrugged his shoulders. 'It's a good job I didn't listen to *you* then.'

Mikey stared at Oswald. 'What have you done?'

Oswald did a little jig to show his excitement. 'I took a video of the farm and surrounding countryside. I then sent it to Adam to show his grandfather. Adam knows what you're trying to achieve here, but he guessed it would take a while to grow the business. Mr Wensley's impressed with your ideas and wants to help.'

Sasha took the lead. 'There's lots to think about, but we must deal with one thing at a time. We should offer Mr Wensley a meal when he arrives *and* make sure he's happy about where we're placing his wife's piano.'

Mikey's head spun around. 'Where can we put the piano?'

Rafferty had a suggestion, 'In the living room. It's large enough.'

Lawrie held his hands in the air. 'It won't fit through the front door.'

Oswald shrugged. 'Maybe you can take a window out.'

Sasha wanted to sink into a hole. This mess had been created because of her. A grand piano on a farm didn't work. She wanted to cry with embarrassment *and* because Grandpa Wilf would soon be on a train on his way back to Durham. She was dealing with too many emotions at once.

Lawrie placed an arm around Sasha's shoulders while kissing the top of her head. 'Don't worry. We'll find a solution. We can do anything now that we're together.'

Oswald raised an eyebrow at Rafferty before staring at Mikey, who smiled and gave a thumbs-up sign. Well, well, well. This weekend was proving to be full of surprises!

Rafferty had a suggestion, 'Why don't we take Mr Wensley to the pub for lunch? That will take the burden off Sasha.'

Lawrie glanced at the earrings in his hand before passing them to his girlfriend. 'Great idea. You can wear these. That was a very kind thought of Moira's; they're obviously for you.'

Sasha took hold of the silver earrings in the shape of pianos. Her eyes widened. 'I saw these in the jewellery shop in Market Furnley. Moira didn't make them, she bought them.'

Mikey shrugged. 'Maybe she just wanted to buy you a present for teaching Tommy the piano.'

Sasha shook her head. 'Moira's craftier than you give her credit for. She's trying to spook me out.'

Oswald laughed. 'Why would she want to do that?'

'To get her foot in the door at the farm.'

Lawrie raised his eyebrows. 'But you've been encouraging us to employ her.'

Sasha sighed. 'I know, but things are different now. Moira has access to the internet. She must know about St Pancras and the Wensley. I'm not safe here anymore.'

Oswald linked his arm through Sasha's. 'You're perfectly safe. You were running away from the paparazzi and your father. They're both linked, and Mr Wensley has snuffed them out. Besides, if Moira knows you're a superstar, she's not let on to the villagers.

We've not seen autograph hunters lurking in the bushes during our strolls around Furnley End. I have a good feeling about Moira. She's only trying to be friendly.'

Rafferty smiled. 'Oswald's right. You've nothing to fear anymore. You should embrace any admiration that comes your way. And trust me, it will. The difference is you're now in charge of your own fate and can move at a pace that suits you.'

Sasha felt a tremendous sense of relief. Too much had happened at once, and she hadn't had time to sit back and take it all in. She tucked her hair behind her ears and put the earrings in. 'I'd best wear these, then. We may bump into Moira in the village at lunchtime.'

27

LUNCH AT THE PUB

Mr Wensley cut into his roast beef. 'I must say this is more than acceptable for a village pub. That's a box ticked for your new venture. Your overnight guests will have a fine pub within walking distance from the farm. It's something people look for when booking holidays in rural parts.'

Sasha chewed on a Yorkshire pudding. She was so relieved the piano had a new home. Mr Wensley had suggested his team of piano removal experts put it in one of the empty barns. The piano was placed on some temporary flooring, and guidance was given on keeping the temperature in the barn at the correct level for such a magnificent instrument. It was summer now, so there was time to install heating before the colder weather set in.

At the end of the meal, Mr Wensley placed his

serviette on the table and directed his gaze at Mikey and Lawrie. 'Now, which one of you do I do business with?'

Mikey gulped. 'Both of us.'

Rafferty pushed his chair back. 'We'll leave so you can have a private discussion.'

Mikey glanced at Lawrie. 'There's no need. We're all family here. Sasha, Oswald, and Rafferty have been instrumental in coming up with ideas to help us get *The New Place to Be* off the ground.'

Mr Wensley smiled. 'I like the name.'

Lawrie's eyes lit up. 'Under the banner of *The New Place to Be*, there will be other elements such as *The Piano Place, The Eating Place, The Shopping Place, The Glamping Place, The Community Allotment Place*. Then, at Christmas, we'll have *Santa's Place. The Bed & Breakfast Place* will have to wait for now. We'll need to do some work on the farmhouse before we can offer that.'

Mr Wensley nodded. 'It sounds like you have it all mapped out. I like young people with vision and drive.' Mr Wensley dropped his head. 'I was young once, with lots of ideas. Unfortunately, I didn't have the backing to make things work as quickly as I would have liked.' Mr Wensley raised his head. 'It is with that in mind I'm offering to be an investor in your business.'

Oswald did a little clap, and Sasha and Rafferty remained silent while trying to gauge Mikey and Lawrie's reaction. Mikey stared at Mr Wensley. 'How would that work? What level of interest would we need to pay on the loan? My father never wanted us to get into debt.'

Mr Wensley's eyes clouded over. 'You two boys could do with a break. I know your history. It bothers me that you didn't manage to take a gap year. You came home to be with Mikey's father. I also know that Lawrie spent all his school holidays on the farm while his mother built her call centre business. I want to help by giving you an interest-free loan. You can pay me back as and when the profits start to come in.'

There were tears in Sasha's eyes as Mikey and Lawrie stood up to shake hands with Mr Wensley. Mikey was speechless, so Lawrie spoke on behalf of both of them, 'Thank you so much. We won't disappoint you, and we'll recommend the Wensley International Hotel to all our guests.'

Mr Wensley smiled. 'I should hope so. We'll be promoting *The New Place to Be* from London. Just make sure you think big. I wouldn't want you to lose out on business if you don't have the capacity to cope. Send me the details of your business bank account, and I'll transfer a lump sum. If you need more, you only need to ask.'

On her way out of the pub, Sasha noticed Moira sitting in a corner of the room. She raised her sherry glass and smiled. She looked so much nicer when she smiled. Sasha touched an earring and mouthed the words: 'Thank you.' This time, Sasha smiled at Moira, who blushed.

On the walk back to the farm, Mr Wensley spoke to Sasha, 'I'm disappointed things didn't work out between you and Adam, but I can quite see that Lawrie is more suited to you. Your grandfather told me *you've* not had an easy time either. I enjoyed my conversation with Wilf. Please let him know he can stay at the Wensley again at any time free of charge.'

Sasha couldn't believe the generosity of this tall, white-haired gentleman. 'I want to thank you for whatever you did to sort out my father. I don't need to know the details. I'm just pleased he's out of my life again.'

Mr Wensley lowered his eyes. 'Ted's a fool to have lost you. If you ever need any fatherly advice, just call me.' Sasha didn't know what to say to that. Mr Wensley then glanced sideways at her. 'Adam told me about the ten thousand pounds. Please tell me you've spent it. Wilf went through great distress getting you to accept it.'

Sasha hadn't told anyone about this yet, so Mr Wensley was the first to hear, 'I've spent lots of it, and

I know what I'm going to spend the rest on.'

'May I ask what?'

'I'm going to take Grandpa Wilf on a cruise just as soon as I've got him a passport.'

Mr Wensley smiled. 'How wonderful. Wilf will be delighted. You're a good girl, Sasha. I can't wait to hear of your progress. I'll keep an eye on things from afar; remember, I'm only a phone call away.'

Back at the farm, the piano removal experts were climbing into their vehicles. 'We've just finished, Mr Wensley. She's been tuned and is ready to go.'

Mr Wensley held out his arm, and Sasha took hold of it as he guided her to her seat. 'Do you have a special request, Mr Wensley?'

'How about *Moon River* from *Breakfast at Tiffany's*? It was my wife's favourite.'

Sasha placed her fingers on the keys and began to play. Mr Wensley turned to Oswald. 'It's incredible that Sasha doesn't need to read sheet music. She plays from memory. The girl is truly gifted.'

Oswald held a hand to his heart. 'I know.'

The farm hands reached for their phones, and before long, most of the villagers were making their way up the riverbank to the farm.

Lawrie's phone rang, it was Moira. 'Moira! How did you get hold of my number?'

'Sharon gave it to me.'

Lawrie gulped. 'Why are you calling?'

'Because we've heard Sasha's playing the piano. Can you keep her going until we get there? We're all heading up from the village. It's not often we get the chance of a free concert.' Moira paused to think. 'The nearest we get is the odd soloist in church on a Sunday, and most of the time, I put my fingers in my ears.'

Lawrie laughed. 'Well, we look forward to seeing you all at the farm. There's no need to rush. Sasha will be playing all night.'

Lawrie updated his friends on the imminent invasion. Mr Wensley rubbed his hands together. 'There's nothing I like more than a party. Bring your best wine up from the cellar, and we can let our hair down.'

Mikey broke the bad news. 'We don't have a wine cellar.'

Mr Wensley took his phone out of his pocket. 'My chauffeur is on his way down from London to collect me. I'll ask him to go to the pub first to buy provisions to feed and water the whole village. I take it they have nuts?'

28

TWO DAYS BEFORE CHRISTMAS

The grand opening of *The New Place to Be* had been delayed until Christmas Eve. The building work had taken longer than planned, with the extra work necessitated by Mr Wensley's "go big, not small" advice. Planning approval had to be obtained for an annexe to the farmhouse, which would contain four en-suite bedrooms and a dining room for Bed & Breakfast guests.

The six Glamping Huts also needed planning permission for a shower and toilet block. There was no objection from the villagers to the extra traffic that would undoubtedly pass through the village centre. Moira looked forward to working with Chloe in the farm shop and cafeteria. Sharon had been recruited as a full-time cleaner, and Tommy came to play on the farm after school with the added attraction of free piano lessons from Sasha.

Blake and Kerstin waited at Kings Cross station for Grandpa Wilf to arrive on the train from Durham. Kerstin spotted him first. 'Grandpa Wilf! You look so well; you've even got a tan.'

Grandpa Wilf did a little jig. 'That cruise did me the world of good. Sasha says she'll take me on another one next year.'

Mr Wensley arrived at the farm by chauffeur. He was looking forward to seeing the developments which had taken place over the last six months. There was a rugged sign outside the entrance to the farm which read:

WENSLEY FARM

FURNLEY END

Home to *The New Place to Be*

Mikey and Lawrie waited at the gate to greet their investor. Mikey shook Mr Wensley's hand. 'My dad could never think of a good name for the farm. We've only ever been known as "Furnley End Farm". We thought "Wensley Farm" had a ring to it. It twins us with the Wensley International. We haven't changed the name officially. We wanted to know your thoughts first.'

Mr Wensley took his silk handkerchief out of his pocket and blew his nose. 'I have no objection. In fact, I'm honoured. You boys have exceeded my expectations.'

Lawrie laughed. 'You'd best come and look around before saying that.'

Mr Wensley walked up the drive to the farmhouse with Mikey and Lawrie. It was getting dark, and twinkling fairy lights lit up the trees. A huge Christmas tree stood proudly outside the farmhouse, and Mikey smiled. 'My father planted that years ago. We never bothered to decorate it after it got so big. It took too much electricity, but this year is different.' Mikey handed Mr Wensley a remote control. 'If you press that button there, you can officially turn on the lights.'

Mr Wensley pressed the button, and the enormous tree lit up with all the colours of the rainbow. Lawrie placed an arm around Mikey. 'Your dad would have been so proud of you.'

Mikey looked up at the darkening sky. The first stars were twinkling, and he turned to face Lawrie. 'Dad will be looking down on us. He'll be proud of you, too.'

Mr Wensley looked to the sky. He hoped his wife approved of what he'd done with her beloved piano. As if on cue, the sound of music coming from *The Piano*

Place made him jump. Mrs Wensley always played *Silent Night* at Christmas. He took a deep breath; that was a sign she was happy. Mr Wensley rubbed his hands together before turning to Mikey and Lawrie. 'Now, show me around. I'm most interested to see what you've done with the Glamping Huts. Do they have heating at this time of the year?'

Oswald and Rafferty didn't have the roof of their BMW down on this occasion. There was a chill in the air, and Oswald was sure it would snow. Rafferty parked outside the farmhouse. 'There you are. I got us here before the weather turned bad.'

Oswald's eyes sparkled. 'Snow isn't bad once you've reached your destination.'

Kerstin phoned Sasha, 'We're five minutes away.'

Sasha jumped off the piano stool. 'OK, I'll meet you outside the farmhouse.'

Lawrie explained where all the guests would be sleeping, 'Mr Wensley and Grandpa Wilf are in *The Bed & Breakfast Place,* and Kerstin, Blake, Oswald, Rafferty, and Adam are in *The Glamping Place.*'

Oswald looked around. 'Where's Adam? I've not seen him yet.'

Mr Wensley advised the whereabouts of his grandson, 'Adam is at the Rugby Club Christmas Party.

He'll be travelling down tomorrow.'

Kerstin whispered to Chloe, 'Best keep a wide berth from Adam. He's got a different girl on his arm each week. Don't forget he started with me and moved on to Sasha. You'll be next.'

Chloe giggled. 'He won't get a chance with me. I'm more than happy with Mikey.'

With all the guests unpacked and assembled in the farmhouse, Chloe advised the menu option for tonight, 'We're having tapas!'

Grandpa Wilf raised his eyebrows at Mr Wensley, who chuckled. 'Don't worry. I'm sure there's a good selection. Just aim for the patatas bravas; that's a safe one.'

'Patatas, what?'

'Potatoes in a tomato sauce. Watch what I choose. You won't go wrong.'

The friends had divided the tapas menu between them, and each cooked a selection of dishes in the farmhouse kitchen. Kerstin and Blake offered to keep the guests supplied with drinks, and Oswald noticed an old record player in the living room. He was in his element as he searched through a pile of records and found a Christmas one. Soon, the farmhouse was filled with the sound of *White Christmas* by *Bing Crosby*.

Grandpa Wilf and Mr Wensley sat in front of a roaring fire, sharing stories about cruising, and Rafferty looked up at the sky. Tiny snowflakes were floating around. He sipped his mulled wine. Oswald may get his dream of a white Christmas after all.

With the tapas selection displayed on food warmers on the dining room table, everyone took their seats. Mr Wensley raised his wineglass. 'I would like to propose a toast to the fine young people of Wensley Farm. I am proud to class you all as friends. Over the last six months, your achievements have brought me much intrigue and joy.'

Grandpa Wilf tapped his glass with a knife. 'Hear! Hear! I second that. You've given us oldies a new lease of life.'

There was laughter around the table as the friends tucked into their meal. Fifteen minutes later, the doorbell rang. Lawrie jumped up. 'I'll answer it.'

Moira stood outside with snow in her hair. 'I walked from the village in case we get snowed in. I couldn't be late for the big day tomorrow.'

Lawrie took Moira's carrier bags and led her to *The Glamping Place*. 'You can use Hut Number Six. It was very kind of you to turn up in good time. There's a selection of drinks in the fridge, and I'll bring you over some left-over tapas in half an hour or so.'

Moira beamed. 'That's very kind of you. I've been given good instructions on how to work the heating.' Moira tapped her nose. 'I'll keep myself scarce so we don't ruin the secret.'

Lawrie walked back into the dining room to the sound of laughter. He smiled. 'What's so funny?'

Sasha giggled. 'It's Grandpa Wilf. He's never eaten an olive before. He thought it was a grape. You should have seen his face!'

Grandpa Wilf placed his empty wine glass on the table. 'Now, now. Less of the frivolity at my expense. I need a top-up before I tackle the next delicacy. Just in case I need to wash it down.'

Mikey turned to Lawrie. 'Who was at the door?'

Lawrie winked. 'Santa. He's arrived early.'

29

THE GRAND OPENING

It was Christmas Eve, and *The New Place to Be* was preparing to welcome its first guests. Today's main attraction was horse-drawn carriage rides around the farm to visit *Santa's Place*. Two carriages were decorated with winter foliage and fairy lights, and the horses wore sleigh bells. Four farm hands had volunteered to wear Elf outfits to drive the carriages of excited children around the farm on their way to see Santa.

There was just a light covering of snow on the ground, and Mr Wensley was relieved the roads weren't too bad for Adam's journey to the farm from London. Chloe had enlisted the help of Kerstin, Blake, Lawrie and Mikey in the cafeteria and farm shop, and Sasha was in *The Piano Place* with the church choir for a carol concert. Mr Wensley and Grandpa Wilf sat in the front row in readiness for the performance to commence.

Kerstin saw Adam's car pulling up outside the farmhouse. She ran out of the cafeteria. 'Have you got them?'

Adam smiled. 'I certainly have. I don't know why people leave things until the last minute. I had to lie to my grandfather about going to a Rugby Club Christmas party last night.'

Kerstin sighed. 'Well, let's just hope it goes to plan today. I, personally, think it's a ridiculous idea.'

It was one-thirty, and Lawrie toured the farm to check everything was in place for the gates to open at two o'clock. The only thing missing was Santa. Lawrie rushed over to Hut Number Six. Moira was fast asleep in her bed. There was an empty bottle of wine on the floor, and Lawrie regretted suggesting Moira helped herself to the drinks in the fridge. He grabbed hold of the bag containing Santa's costume and headed straight for Adam. 'Come to *Santa's Place*. You're needed urgently.'

Sharon was surprised to see the burly rugby player with large, tattooed arms pulling on her mother's outfit. *She* was dressed as a festive cowgirl and in charge of handing out presents to the children. The cowgirl bent over to straighten the sacks and giggled when Santa winked at her. Sharon didn't know what had happened to her mother, but she wasn't concerned. This afternoon was going to be much more fun than she had expected. Adam wondered why there was a cowgirl in *Santa's place*, but he wasn't complaining!

The cuckoo clock, which had been banished to *The Piano Place*, sounded twice, much to Grandpa Wilf's delight and Mr Wensley's amusement. Sasha's fingers touched the piano keys, and the concert began.

Kerstin was out of breath when she ran back into the cafeteria. Despite her efforts to resist, Chloe insisted she change into the same outfit as her and Sasha. Moira had made three full-length red velvet dresses with long sleeves and white faux fur around the necklines. Sasha had paid for the material with the last of the cash.

Things were going well in *Santa's Place*. Adam could lower his voice to a much deeper level than Moira would have been able to achieve, even though she'd been practising for the last four weeks.

Mark was looking after Tommy this afternoon, and he stepped off the horse-drawn carriage while holding the young boy's hand. Tommy grinned as he looked around at the other children, then held up his hand to whisper in Mark's ear, 'It's not the real Santa. It's my Granny. I've seen her practising.'

Mark couldn't dispute what Tommy had

witnessed with his own eyes, so he whispered back, 'Well, let's not tell the other children. The real Santa will be getting on his sleigh now up in Lapland. He's going to be very busy tonight.'

Tommy waited patiently in line until it was *his* turn to go inside the barn with the sign: *Santa's Place*.

When the child before him came out holding a present, Tommy bounded inside and jumped on Santa's lap. 'Granny! I know it's you.'

Sharon threw a hand to her mouth, and Adam chuckled before speaking in a deep voice, 'Well, well, well, young man. I'm sorry to disappoint you, but I'm not your grandmother. I've come all this way to see you from Lapland, and today's my busiest day of the year.' Adam elaborated, 'The reindeer are hiding in one of the other barns on this splendid farm. They're eating lots of moss to keep their strength up. But don't go telling anyone. That's our secret.'

Tommy had turned white; his mouth was open, and he couldn't move. Mark walked over and lifted him into his arms. 'There's no need to be afraid, Tommy. Santa's been very kind to make all the effort to come here this afternoon. Aren't you the lucky one?'

Mark winked at Adam and carried Tommy to Sharon to receive his present. Moira was standing outside the barn when Mark and Tommy appeared.

Tommy stared at her. 'The real Santa came to see me. Mummy's in the barn helping him. She's giving out the presents.'

Moira turned in search of Lawrie. She didn't want to lose her job over this. She needed to offer her help elsewhere to make up for being late on such a special day. She'd had the best intentions by arriving in good time. Unfortunately, she'd needed a bottle of wine to wash down the tapas meal. She was sure the grapes were dodgy.

By five o'clock, the crowd had begun to disperse. Moira was pleased to have been of help in the farm shop. She'd released Lawrie, who had something important to do. *Santa's Place* had a "CLOSED" sign hanging outside and a party going on inside. Mikey had taken the remaining festive food and drink from the cafeteria and farm shop to the barn so that today's helpers could let their hair down. Grandpa Wilf and Mr Wensley tucked into mince pies while Adam entertained them with stories of his eventful afternoon.

Sasha, Chloe and Kerstin were in the farmhouse. They had been told to stay in the living room with Oswald and Rafferty, who were standing beside the record player. It had been snowing all day, and the girls warmed their hands by the roaring fire, wondering what was happening. Kerstin was in a bad mood. 'This is ridiculous. I'm a spare part. I'm not waiting in here any longer. I'll be in the kitchen if you need me.'

At the sight of the living room door opening, Oswald started the music. The farmhouse was soon filled with the sound of *Andy Williams* singing *It's the Most Wonderful Time of the Year*. Lawrie and Mikey had changed into suits, and they walked up to their girlfriends before asking, 'May we have this dance?'

Kerstin tried to escape past Blake, who was in the doorway. Blake had also changed into a suit. He blocked her way. 'Where do you think *you're* going?'

Kerstin blinked away a tear. 'As far away as possible. I'm the odd one out.'

Blake held his hand out. 'May I have this dance?'

Kerstin wished the floor would open up and swallow her. She was even more annoyed now that Blake was being so inconsiderate. He knew the plan, and Kerstin didn't feature in it. Blake pulled a small box out of his jacket pocket. 'You won't get this until you've danced with me. I missed out on all the fun at St Pancras station. I believe you were dancing with Adam on that occasion.'

Kerstin stood in stunned silence, so Blake took her into his arms. 'Hold on tight. We can't let the others have all the fun.' Kerstin could see flashes of Sasha and Chloe as Blake spun her around; her friends were giddy and excited. Oswald and Rafferty were standing next to the record player with grins plastered across their faces, and Kerstin could hardly breathe in case this was a joke.

After three Christmas songs, the music stopped. Lawrie and Mikey whisked Sasha and Chloe upstairs to their rooms to reveal their surprises in private, and Blake winked at Oswald and Rafferty. 'Excuse us, we're just nipping outside. We won't be long.'

Blake bent down on one knee in the snow. 'Will you marry me, Kerstin? I doubt I'll ever find a more beautiful, obnoxious woman to grow old with. You're quite right about being the odd one out. Sasha and Chloe's fiancés will be kneeling down on carpets. I'll be the only one with wet trousers.'

Kerstin was in shock. 'But we arranged for this to be a surprise for Sasha and Chloe. We've kept it a secret for the last two weeks. I had to get their ring sizes by playing a silly game of who had the fattest fingers by sticking our ring fingers through a piece of card.'

Blake's eyes twinkled. 'I know. And you did an excellent job. I was able to tell what size *your* ring finger was as well. I was surprised Chloe's fingers are the fattest.'

Kerstin giggled. She'd been surprised about that, too. She held out her hand for Blake to slide the oval diamond ring onto her slim finger. 'Good choice.'

'Does that mean the answer is "yes"?'

'Of course, it means "yes". I don't feel like the odd one out anymore. It's bad enough the girls live together on the farm. I was struggling to handle the fact that they would both be engaged, and I wasn't. That was just too much to take.'

Blake stood up and pulled Kerstin into his arms. 'Too much talking.'

The front door opened, and Sasha and Chloe stood in the hallway holding out their left hands. They both giggled. 'What's yours like?'

Kerstin held out her left hand, too. 'It's perfect. I always wanted an oval diamond.'

Adam ran down the snow-covered path from *Santa's Place* to the sight of smiling faces. 'I see it's all gone to plan. You have *me* to thank for that. I was in Hatton Garden this morning collecting the rings. I hope that puts me in line for being Best Man to all of you. It was a scary task; I was walking around London carrying a bag worth a fortune.'

The girls all looked at each other before laughing; they knew the feeling about walking around London carrying a fortune. Blake's sports bag sprang to mind.

Adam wiped the snow from his shoulders. 'Anyway, I just popped over here to borrow the record player. There's quite a party starting at *Santa's Place*. The farm hands said Mikey's dad had some great line dancing records we could use.'

With Mikey's approval, Oswald searched for the line dancing records while Rafferty unplugged the record player.

Adam grinned. 'Well, I'll make my way back there then. It would be good to bring a few more beers over and some bottles of wine. Moira's recovered from earlier, and she's thirsty. She's also asking if you have any more olives. She thought they were grapes. Wilf said he made the same mistake yesterday.'

Everyone burst out laughing, and Lawrie smiled at Sasha. 'Let's go and tell your grandfather our happy news.'

Sasha smiled back. 'It will make his Christmas.'

Adam turned to head back before glancing over his shoulder. 'Don't be too long, or you'll miss the festive cowgirl strutting her stuff. Sharon's very popular with the locals. You should see her outfit. Her little white boots are really,' Adam winked at the boys, 'cute!'

Sasha raised an eyebrow. 'Where's Tommy?'

'Mark took him back to the vicarage. He was in a state of shock from seeing the real Santa. Sharon's promised to pick him up by six-thirty so she can take him home to bed.'

Blake strode down the hallway towards the kitchen. 'I'll help carry provisions. Just load me up with bags. Be quick, or we'll miss the festive cowgirl.' Lawrie and Mikey dashed after him.

Oswald and Rafferty squeezed past the girls with the record player and records. 'We'd best get a move on. We wouldn't want to keep the line dancers waiting.'

The girls heard laughter coming from the kitchen. They crept down the hallway to see their fiancés, beers in hand, talking about Sharon.

Mikey let out a sigh of relief. 'It's been worrying me for years that Sharon would get her claws into Lawrie.'

Lawrie nodded. 'I know she's had a thing for me.'

Sasha glared at her friends.

Blake slapped Lawrie on the back. 'She's quite a looker.'

Kerstin's eyes were ablaze.

Mikey finished his beer before placing it in a bottle bin. 'My dad always hoped *I'd* marry Sharon.'

Tears welled in Chloe's eyes.

Lawrie and Blake placed their empty bottles in the bin, too.

Mikey began to load boxes and bags with provisions from the fridge. 'Mind you, if my dad had met Chloe, he'd have been thrilled to have her as a daughter-in-law.'

Lawrie placed an arm around Mikey's shoulders. 'He certainly would. He'd have loved Sasha, too. Your dad took me under his wing; I always considered him a father figure.'

Sasha and Chloe hugged one another.

Blake sensed they had listeners in the corridor, and he couldn't resist winding up *his* nosey fiancée. 'Now, Kerstin's another matter. She's a bit feisty at times.'

Kerstin burst into the kitchen, and Blake winked at her. 'She's also kind-hearted, intelligent, beautiful, and the perfect match for me.'

Kerstin huffed. 'We'd best get a move on. We'll never hear the end of it if you boys miss the cowgirl in all her glory. We'll head on over to get you front-row seats.'

Kerstin closed the kitchen door behind her before smiling at her friends. 'We've all done well. Let's go and party. It sounds like Santa will need rescuing from the cowgirl – or vice versa.'

The friends hitched up their dresses as they ran through the snow in the knowledge that it had taken just six months to achieve their dreams. Little had Chloe and Kerstin known when they bought Sasha the train ticket to Durham that their act of kindness would change all their lives beyond belief.

Kerstin frowned at Sasha. 'Did you pay us for that train ticket we bought?'

Sasha giggled. 'I don't think I did.'

****

Printed in Great Britain
by Amazon